What Readers
the Samantha

"*Bad Connection* is a terrific story for anyone who loves supernatural fiction. My daughters are going to be arguing over who gets to read it first." WITHDRAWN

RANDY INGERMANSON, winner of two Christy Awards
and author of *Double Vision*

"God does what He wills and cannot be manipulated. This is the sound doctrinal message for Melody Carlson's book *Bad Connection*. Writing about a spiritual gift we rarely see today was risky, but handled so well I would encourage any teen (or their parents) to read this book. I was reminded that we are not to be afraid of God's more unusual gifts, but to allow Him to use them in our lives."

LISSA HALLS JOHNSON, creator of the Brio Girls series,
co-author of *A Full House of Growing Pains*

"Bravo to Melody Carlson for creating a wonderful, engaging character who is just like our daughters and the teens in our church. Yet, she's gifted with visions from God. After eighteen years in youth ministry and watching the world present an enticing display of the supernatural, I'm thrilled to see Christian fiction address this issue, letting teens know that greater is He that is in you, than he that is in the world."

RACHEL HAUCK, author of *Lost in NashVegas*

"*Bad Connection* has it all: suspense, a ripped-from-the-headlines plot, and characters you'd find in any high school. It's a novel I'd definitely recommend to my teenage grand-daughters and their friends."

PATRICIA H. RUSHFORD, author of the
Jennie McGrady Mysteries

the secret life of Samantha
McGregor
BOOK TWO

beyond
reach

a novel

melody
carlson

Multnomah Books

BEYOND REACH
published by Multnomah Books
A division of Random House, Inc.

and in association with the literary agency of Sara A. Fortenberry

© 2007 by Carlson Management Co., Inc.

International Standard Book Number: 1-59052-693-7

Cover design by David Carlson Design

Cover photo by Steve Gardner, www.shootpw.com

Unless otherwise indicated, Scripture quotations are from:

The Message

" 1993, 1994, 1995, 1996, 2000, 2001, 2002

Used by permission of NavPress Publishing Group

Multnomah is a trademark of Multnomah Publishers,
and is registered in the U.S. Patent and Trademark Office.
The colophon is a trademark of Multnomah Publishers.

Printed in the United States of America

For information:

MULTNOMAH BOOKS
12265 ORACLE BOULEVARD, SUITE 200
COLORADO SPRINGS, CO 80921

LIBRARY OF CONGRESS CATALOGING-IN-PUBLICATION DATA

Carlson, Melody.

Beyond reach : a novel / Melody Carlson.

p. cm. -- (The secret life of Samantha Mcgregor ; bk. 2)

Summary: Samantha has a gift from God that makes her see visions of crimes and impending disasters, and she struggles to use this special ability to help people and to glorify God.

ISBN 1-59052-693-7

[1. Christian life—Fiction. 2. Visions—Fiction. 3. Suicide—Fiction. 4. Death—Fiction. 5. High schools—Fiction. 6. Schools—Fiction.] I. Title.

PZ7.C216637Bey 2007

[Fic]—dc22

2006034482

07 08 09 10 11 12 13—10 9 8 7 6 5 4 3 2 1

Author's Note

I normally don't include a letter in my books, but because The Secret Life of Samantha McGregor series treads on some new territory, I want to make a few things as clear as possible. First of all, this book is *fiction*—it's simply a story that's meant to entertain and to possibly point out some spiritual truths—but it is *not* a theological study on the proper use of the gifts of the Holy Spirit. While I do believe in the gifts of the Holy Spirit and that God wants all of us to do many wonderful things, I also realize that Samantha's gift, her ability to receive dreams and visions from God, is extremely rare and unique—but it does make for a good story!

Second, my hope is that you won't envy Samantha's unusual gift or seek it for yourself, since that would be totally wrong! Don't forget that God is the giver of every good and perfect gift, and *He's* the One who decides who gets what and when it's appropriate to use. If you go around searching for your own gifts, you can put yourself at serious risk. Satan masquerades as an angel of light and delights in tricking those who look for gifts in the wrong places. Don't let that be you.

More than anything, I hope you'll follow Samantha's example by seeking out God and a committed relationship with Him. I hope you'll desire to walk closely with God every day, to make Him your best friend, and to be ready for whatever adventures and gifts He has in store for you. Just make sure they come from God!

And finally, remember that the Bible is our ultimate source for answers to all of life's questions. That's why I've included more Scripture in this series than usual. Also, please check out the resources and discussion questions in the back of this book.

I pray that this fictional journey will draw your heart closer to God and that He will be your lifeline—for today and for always!

Best blessings!

Melody Carlson

A Word from Samantha

The first time it happened, I thought it was pretty weird but kind of cool. The second time it happened, I got a little freaked. The third time it happened, I became seriously scared and had sort of a meltdown. That's when my mom decided to send me to a shrink. She thought I was going crazy. And I thought she was right for a change.

Turns out it was just God. Okay, not just God. Because, believe me, God is way more than just anything. Still, it was hard to explain this weird phenomenon to my mom or the shrink or anyone. It still is. Other than my best friend, Olivia, I don't think most people really get me.

But that's okay, because I know that God gets me. For that reason, I try to keep this part of my life under wraps. For the most part anyway.

A Word from the Word…

And ye shall know that I am in the midst of Israel, and that I am the LORD your God, and none else: and my people shall never be ashamed. And it shall come to pass afterward, that I will pour out my spirit upon all flesh; and your sons and your daughters shall prophesy, your old men shall dream dreams, your young men shall see visions: And also upon the servants and upon the handmaids in those days will I pour out my spirit. (Joel 2:27–29, KJV)

One

Mission accomplished. Kayla Henderson is safe. After a typical holiday delay, the plane has just taken off from Phoenix, and Ebony and I are flying back to Oregon now—just in time for Christmas.

After discovering there's no in-flight movie, I recline my seat, close my eyes, and slowly exhale. I am so ready to kick back for a while. Our flight won't arrive in Portland for a couple of hours, perfect for a nice long snooze. It looks like Ebony is one step ahead of me. I let out a deep sigh and feel myself sinking into a state of what I hope will turn into comatose slumber…

I'm barely out when I feel a sharp metallic jab on my elbow and look up to see the stainless steel beverage cart attempting to rattle its way past me.

"Excuse me, miss," says the blond flight attendant. "Your arm is in the way."

"Sorry." I pull in my arm and sit up straighter, rubbing the sore spot where the cart rammed me. You'd think they'd be more careful with those things. Anyway I'm wide-awake now. So much for my nap, although it looks like most of the other passengers are fast asleep. Lucky them.

Melody Carlson

I watch the blond flight attendant slowly working her cart up the aisle, and I can't help but think that it must be a fairly boring job. Not only does her career seem somewhat tedious, but I've noticed that a lot of the passengers, particularly during the holidays, can be pretty rude and impatient.

She parks her cart at the front of the plane, then pours a cup of coffee, sets it on the little tray, and walks back a few rows. Then she leans over to give it to a dark-haired man sitting on the aisle. As he reaches for the cup, the little tray tips slightly and the coffee cup slips off and empties its hot contents right over the poor man's front. He instantly leaps to his feet and attempts to brush the brown liquid off his white shirt, which now looks less than white. He's saying something, which I can't hear, but I see his arms flailing about, and it's obvious he is angry about this little incident.

Naturally, the flight attendant apologizes profusely, attempting to dry him off with some beverage napkins. Finally she ushers him up by the bathrooms, where I assume she will find a towel to dry him off. Poor guy. Not only did he get scalded, it looks like his stained shirt is sopping wet too. She really should be more careful.

Then, just as I assume the little scene has settled down, the man suddenly grabs the flight attendant by her arm, and I'm thinking that this is turning into one serious case of air rage. I start to nudge Ebony in case this goes any further. I know that as a cop she's trained for this sort of thing. But in that same instant, the angry man wraps his other arm tightly around the flight attendant's neck, almost like he intends on strangling her.

Her frightened eyes are bulging, as if she can barely breathe. But the worst part is that I notice a silver glint in his other hand. He has a knife! And it actually looks like he's threatening to kill her. All this over a cup of coffee? I give Ebony a sharp nudge with my elbow. This is crazy!

"Nobody move!" yells the dark-haired man in a strong Middle Eastern accent. *"I have a bomb!"* Just then I hear a woman scream from the back of the plane, and I turn my head in time to see another man, who also appears to be Middle Eastern, running up the aisle toward us. I glance at Ebony and she's wide-awake, looking just as shocked as I am.

I don't say a word, but I wonder if she can help, although I know her handgun is packed in her carry-on bag, which is stowed a few seats behind us in the crowded overhead storage. Not exactly easy to access without being observed.

Then I hope perhaps the man moving down the aisle is actually an air marshal who is armed and prepared to stop this crazy thing, although his appearance suggests just the opposite. He's only a few feet away when I notice that he's also armed with a knife! I'm about to stick my foot into the aisle to trip him when I feel Ebony give me a nudge from the other side.

And that's when I wake up!

"Are you okay, Samantha?"

I blink and study Ebony's concerned bronze face for a moment, then turn back to look around the plane. All is calm and appears perfectly normal. And everyone is still asleep. No knives, no bombs, no mad terrorists running down the aisle screaming…just peace and quiet. "I was asleep," I say, feeling stupid.

"Bad dream?" Ebony asks with sympathy.

I nod and take in a deep breath, slowly exhaling. "Yeah, thank goodness. It was just a dream." I sort of chuckle when I think of how freaked I'd just been. All because of a silly dream. But then I notice the same blond flight attendant up front, and she's pouring a cup of coffee for a dark-haired guy, and suddenly I'm not sure. Was it just a dream?

"Ebony," I say with alarm. "It was a dream…but maybe not *just* a dream." Then I quickly retell her my dream. But as I stumble over the words, trying to get it all out before it actually unfolds for real, my eyes stay locked on the scene up in front. My heart is pounding frantically, and I'm almost afraid to look as the flight attendant lowers the hot beverage tray and the dark-haired man simply takes the coffee without any problems.

"It didn't spill," I whisper to Ebony.

"Is that the same man as in your dream?"

I consider this, trying to remember the exact details. "No. The man in my dream was in the third row from the front. And he didn't have a bald spot on the back of his head either. Plus his hair was a bit longer, with a little bit of curl on the ends." I close my eyes, focusing on the images from my dream. "He had on a white shirt, and as I recall it wasn't tucked in. The guy up there has on a suit jacket."

"Do you see the guy from your dream anywhere on the plane, perhaps in another seat?"

I glance around then shake my head. "And that elderly woman is sitting in the seat he was in in my dream." I sigh with relief. "See, it really was just a dream."

"What about the other man? The one running up the aisle? Do you see him?"

I consider this. "I can't really see clear to the back of the plane."

"Want to take a walk?"

"Sure." So I unbuckle and get out of my seat. Everything's still pretty quiet, and no one seems to wonder why I'm going to the rear of the plane to use the restroom when there's a perfectly good one much closer in the front.

Still, I slowly walk down the aisle, carefully but inconspicuously checking out all the passengers. Most of them are sleeping or reading or listening to headphones. I'm sure they're on their way to visit relatives or returning home for the holidays. And not one of them looks anything like either of the terrorist men in my dream. As I recall, the guy in the back was wearing an olive green sports jacket. Soccer I think. Probably for an international team. His hair was cut shorter than his cohort, combed smooth.

It was only a dream. Why obsess? I return to my seat.

"See anyone suspicious?" Ebony asks as I sit back down.

"No," I tell her as I buckle my seat belt again. "It really was *just* a dream."

She smiles and pats my hand. "Well, thank God for that."

I nod. "Yeah. How creepy was that dream though? Terrorists on Christmas Eve? Really sad timing, huh?"

She sighs. "Well, it could happen. Terrorists like to hit where and when it hurts."

I try not to think about that as we both settle back into our seats. Whatever my dream was about, it was obviously not about me or this flight. Even so, I pray about it. I ask God to protect all the people traveling during the holidays—to get them safely to their destinations. Then I tell myself to forget about it. God can take care of it much better than I can. And thankfully I finally do fall asleep again.

I wake up to another nudging. It's the blond flight attendant again. Not thumping me with her cart like in my dream, but telling me to put my seat forward. "We're about to land," she says with a smile.

"Thanks." I adjust my seat and look around. Still, all is normal.

Soon we are taxiing, and then we're getting off the plane. The blond flight attendant wishes us a Merry Christmas as we leave.

"Merry Christmas to you too," I say to her, and since the people in front of us aren't moving very fast I ask, "Do you have to work during the holidays?"

"Just the return flight back to Phoenix, and then I'm off until New Year's Day." She smiles happily. "The longest break I've had in years. I even promised to take my five-year-old to Disneyland next week."

"Have fun," I tell her as the line starts to move again.

Then, as we're emerging at the gate, I see something that sends a chill clear to the pit of my stomach. But I pretend like nothing is wrong, walking away from the gate then stopping a couple of gates down.

"Why are you stopping—" Ebony stares at me. "Sam, you look like you just saw a ghost."

"The guys—the ones—you know, in my dream," I manage to stutter.

"Really?"

"The one in the white shirt with the tails out," I say quickly. "And the one in the olive green soccer jacket. Arab-looking." I grab her arm and motion with my eyes toward the seats at the gate we just exited from. "They're on the flight to Phoenix—with the blond flight attendant."

"Third row from the front?" Ebony says quickly. "Aisle seat on the right?"

"Yes."

"I'll go take a quick look. You wait here."

It feels like an hour, but it's really only a couple minutes before Ebony returns. "Let's find security," she says in an urgent voice.

It doesn't take long to find a uniformed guard. Ebony shows him her badge. "We have reason to believe there are terrorists on the next United flight to Phoenix."

He looks appropriately alarmed, immediately gets on his radio, and then directs us to an unmarked door where he pushes a security code. We're ushered into a small office and introduced to Officer Banks, a plainclothes security person who's sitting at a desk with a computer.

"There's no time to explain everything." Ebony shows Officer Banks her badge, then gives quick descriptions of the two dark-haired men, which gate they're waiting at, and which seat the man in the white shirt should be assigned to if my dream is correct.

Officer Banks immediately picks up the phone, dispersing more instructions and details, and then hangs up and just looks at us. I can't tell if he thinks we're kooks or what. Then he asks if we have checked bags, which we don't, and he relays this information to yet another person.

"So, did you get the guys?" I ask. "Are they terrorists?"

"We're checking on them."

"But you won't let them on the flight, will you?" I persist, thinking about the blond flight attendant's plans to take her child to Disneyland next week.

"We'll hold them long enough to do a thorough search," he tells us in a business-as-usual sort of voice. "If we have reason to detain them further, we will."

Then he asks us some questions about ourselves, and Ebony explains how we've been down in Phoenix working on a case with the FBI. But he looks pretty skeptical as he tells us to hand over our photo IDs, which he photocopies. As he's entering this information into his computer, I take out my cell phone and start to dial my mom.

"You'll have to give me that." He holds out his hand. Then he confiscates Ebony's cell phone too, but he allows us each to make one phone call on his landline to inform family and friends of our unfortunate delay.

Shortly after that, a female uniformed officer comes into the office and confiscates our carry-on bags. "For a routine check," we're informed. Then we just sit there in the stuffy little office, listening to elevator-style Christmas music as we wait and wait and wait. Even when we need to use the restroom, we are escorted by the female officer. I am feeling more and more like Ebony and I are the ones being treated like criminals here. What is up with this?

More than that, I'm extremely worried that those two terrorists could be out there running around free, possibly even boarding the plane by now. Or for all I know, maybe they're already in flight, getting ready to blow up the plane.

"Can we go now?" I ask with obvious irritation.

"Not yet," says Banks as he punches something else into his computer keyboard. Maybe he's e-mailing his friends, wishing them happy holidays.

"But it's Christmas Eve," I point out. "How long do you plan on keeping us here anyway?"

"Until I am authorized to release you." He gives me a long, hard look that I suspect is a warning of sorts.

"But we—"

"It's okay, Samantha," Ebony says in a soothing tone. "I'm sure this is simply procedure."

She turns to Officer Banks, handing him what looks like an FBI business card, probably from Tony Mendez, the Phoenix agent in charge of the Kayla Henderson case that we just helped to solve. "If you have doubts about our story, you might want to give this man a call. He can verify who we are."

He peers at the card with a furrowed brow. "You ladies want something to drink?" He sounds a little friendlier now. "Coffee, soda, water?"

We both ask for water, which he sends for, and then we drink it and wait some more. Finally, his phone rings and he listens and nods, and his eyes show that he's actually surprised by something. "Is that so?" He listens some more, glancing at Ebony and me, seemingly impressed, but also a little suspicious. Finally he hangs up.

"Well, I'll be." He places both palms on his desk as he studies the two of us.

"They *were* terrorists?" asks Ebony.

"They don't have all the details just yet, but it seems to be a real possibility." He peers curiously at us. "How did you gals know about this anyway?"

Ebony glances at me. "It's a long story."

"Well, if you ladies want to be home by Christmas, you'd better start telling it to me now." He holds up a small recording device. "And you need to know that this will be recorded."

To my relief, Ebony offers to speak first. She tells him about my special gift—how God gives me visions and dreams that can sometimes be useful in solving criminal cases. Of course, he has a hard time believing what's sounding pretty far-fetched even to my own ears.

After she explains my dream on the plane to him, he picks up the phone and actually manages to connect with Tony. Naturally, we can't hear Tony's end of the conversation, but apparently it's sufficient to verify my "gift," which is feeling more like a curse at the moment.

"So you're like that medium on TV?" Banks finally asks me after he's finished up his little inquisition.

"No," I say quickly and firmly, my exasperation and weariness clearly showing now. "My dreams and visions come from God. I have no control over them, and I am *not* a medium. I'm a Christian who just happens to have a gift." *Thank you very much!*

"God reveals things to Samantha," Ebony explains in a softer tone. "He gives her some important pieces of information. It's because she has a very unique connection to Him. It's hard for others to understand this, but it's simply the way God designed her."

Just then, some other security personnel come into the office to meet us, congratulating us and thanking us for our help. Luggage and phones are returned. But to my dismay, Officer Banks proceeds to tell these people about my gift, and naturally more questions follow. Thankfully, Ebony fields the queries for me. I'm afraid my patience has worn painfully thin—I just want to go home.

"So, you really did catch the guys?" I finally ask Officer Banks. I mean, we heard they were detained and all, but I want to be sure they're really locked up. "The flight's okay and no one's going to be hurt?"

"Don't worry," one of the younger guards assures me. "Those two dudes won't be hurting anyone tonight."

"Unfortunately, there are a bunch of disgruntled passengers who won't be making it to Phoenix tonight either." Then the female security officer briefly explains how the plane and all the checked bags must be moved to a safe and secure place and thoroughly searched. "And with the shortage of flights this time of year, they might not even make it home by tomorrow. I'm afraid this is going to spoil a whole lot of Christmases."

"Not as much as being blown up in the sky would spoil them," Ebony points out.

"I'm curious," I say. "With all the security checks and X-ray machines and stuff...how did those guys get through with bombs and knives?"

"There's more than one way to get down to the gates," says Officer Banks. "Sure, passengers have to go through some tight security, but we also have food service people and various deliveries that come through other avenues. And sometimes passengers, perhaps even our terrorist fellows today, have friends on the inside."

"Friends who can sneak in knives and things," says the young guard.

"Nothing is absolutely certain yet, but there will be a thorough investigation," the female officer assures us.

Then, after asking and answering a few more questions, we are finally allowed to leave the airport.

"Free at last," I say as we head for the parking lot to hunt for Ebony's car. I can hardly believe we parked it there just two days ago, back when we set out on our mission to Phoenix. Was it only this morning that we were out on the desert searching for Kayla and her kidnapper? It seems like two years must've passed since that time. What a day!

"You might've just saved a whole lot of lives tonight, Sam." Ebony opens the trunk of her unmarked police car. We both set our bags inside, and she closes it with a thunk.

"Not me, *God.*"

"Yes, but you were listening, Sam. You were tuned in."

I consider this as she drives us back to Brighton. I suppose I was tuned in. But really, it seemed like I didn't have that much to do with it. I mean, besides being on the receiving end of things. But then I guess that's how it is with God's gifts. They just come—unexpected.

Even so, I'm ready for a little break just now. Or maybe even a big break. I'm not saying I want to tune out completely, but I wouldn't mind a few nights (maybe even a few weeks) of dreamless sleep. I silently beg God to give me some time off during Christmas break—it doesn't seem too much to ask. It's not like I'm telling Him to get lost. I just want Him to leave me alone for a while. Just give me a break. That's all.

TWO

The holidays passed in a surprisingly quiet way. This was partly due to the fact that my brother, Zach, is still in drug rehab up in Washington State.

Mom was a little blue about him being away from home, but I reminded her that it was much better than last Christmas, when Zach was "home" but went on a serious binge during the holidays and we never saw him at all. At least we don't have to be worried about him getting arrested or killed this year since he's locked up, or sort of locked up. His rehab place's philosophy is actually founded on "trust and free will." Let's just hope Zach stays trustworthy and willing long enough to get better.

He called us on Christmas Day, and it sounded like he was doing okay. Sure, he had regular complaints about things like having to get up too early, his neurotic roommate, and the revolving menu... Who wouldn't complain? But for the most part, I think he's sticking to the program. Even so, he's not even halfway finished with his treatment, so I've really been praying for him lately, begging God to help him hang in there—to beat his methamphetamine addiction once and for all. My best friend, Olivia Marsh, has been praying too. She's always been a good prayer partner when it comes to my way-ward brother.

Anyway, I'm thankful for this much-needed calm during Christmas vacation, and I think maybe God realized that I needed a break after all. But the new year has begun and it's time to go back to school. I'm a little concerned about Kayla Henderson. Her story was in both the local and national news on Christmas Day and a few days afterward. At first they ran it as a Christmas miracle story, which it was, and thankfully they didn't give all the details about how she was found or who was involved. So my anonymity seemed safe. As Olivia drives us to school, suddenly I'm worried.

Will Kayla be back in classes today? And if so, will she get to talking and let it out that I played a rather strange role in her rescue down in Arizona?

At the time I told her I was working "undercover" with Ebony and begged her to keep it quiet. But so much has happened since then… What if she forgot? Maybe I should've reminded her about this when we talked on the phone a few days after Christmas. I'd called just to check on how she was doing, and to be honest, it didn't sound like she was doing that great. But I tried to encourage her, and I promised to pray for her. I even invited her to youth group, although she declined, saying she wasn't ready to see people yet.

"You okay, Sam?" Olivia glances at me as she pulls into the school parking lot.

"Yeah." I reach for my bag. "I'm just worried that Kayla might spill the beans about me."

"I thought you had some kind of an arrangement with her." Olivia snags a good parking place and turns off her car. "And seriously, why would she want to talk about all that crud anyway? I mean it's pretty humiliating to her, falling for a cyber jerk like that Colby creep and then actually going down there to meet him. Ugh!" She makes a face. "If I were Kayla, I'd be keeping my mouth shut."

"You're probably right."

Olivia softens. "Just the same, we can look for her, Sam. You could give her a gentle reminder."

"Good idea," I say as we walk across the foggy parking lot. The air feels like it's laced with ice today, and I wish I'd remembered the cashmere gloves Mom gave me for Christmas.

Once inside the building, we head straight for where Olivia thinks Kayla's locker used to be. But we don't see Kayla anywhere. So we walk around, checking out the usual places, and even ask Emma Piscolli, not exactly Kayla's best friend, if she's seen her this morning.

Emma just shakes her head. "And I've been looking for her too. I asked Brittany and Amelia if they'd seen or talked to her, but apparently no one has."

"Why don't we call her cell?" Olivia suggests.

"I don't know her number," I point out.

"I do," says Emma.

"Are you guys talking about Kayla?" asks Kendall Zilcowski.

Now, although Kendall and Kayla couldn't be *any more* different (Kayla being a wild child and Kendall being a wallflower), the two girls had become fairly good friends last fall, back before Kayla went mysteriously missing.

"Yes," I tell Kendall. "Have you seen her?"

"Sure. We hung together during winter break, after Christmas…you know, after she came home from Arizona."

"How's she doing?" asks Olivia.

Kendall makes an uncertain face. "It's not easy…"

"Is she here?" I ask.

Now Kendall shakes her head. "She wasn't ready to come back to school. She's pretty freaked that everyone will treat her weird…you know, because of all the stories that have been in the news. She thinks the whole thing will get blown even more out of proportion with her friends talking about stuff and that everyone will want to know all the gory details about her kidnapper and the murders and all that crud."

I slowly nod. After the capture of Colby Buckley, bits and pieces of the "Internet abductor" story slowly surfaced in the news. We learned how this criminal used the Internet to lure unsuspecting teen girls into his make-believe world with lies and promises and fake photos. Then, after getting them soundly hooked, he would wire them money to come visit. And once he got a girl down there, he would hold her captive and sexually assault her. Then he would brutally murder her and bury her remains in the desert. So far six victims have been identified by their remains. Horrifying stuff.

"I can't blame her," says Olivia. "I wouldn't want every-one staring at me or asking me questions either."

"Exactly," says Kendall. "So she and her mom have decided to move away from Brighton. Kayla plans to dye and cut her hair and use a different name. Hopefully she'll get a fresh start someplace where people aren't as tuned in to the story."

Okay, I feel guilty for being glad about this, because it's a selfish kind of glad. But then I realize that I'm glad for Kayla's sake too. Coming back to Brighton High after everything, well, it would be pretty hard. "I hope she gets some good counseling too," I say as I remember Ebony's concerns.

"She's already going to a counselor," says Kendall. "And I'm sure she'll keep it up. Her mom was adamant about it. In fact, her mom's seeing a counselor too. I guess the one good thing that came out of all this is that Kayla and her mom are working some stuff out now."

"That's worth a lot," I say. Of course, I'm thinking it couldn't possibly be worth all that Kayla's been through—God only knows what that was like—but I'm glad that she and her mom are finally getting along. I vaguely wonder if Mom and I would get closer if I went through something like Kayla's ordeal. No thanks. I know for a fact that I don't want to go there. Not for anything!

"Well, I plan to keep praying for her," announces Olivia.

"Me too," I agree.

"So will I," Kendall says, which surprises me since I wasn't sure that she was a Christian.

"Cool." I decide I should get to know this normally quiet girl a little better.

But the warning bell is ringing now, and since it's the first day back at school, we all skitter away like we don't want to be late for class. As I head for English, I try to remember what we were working on before winter break. I seriously don't understand why our school insists on having four quarters like this. I wish we were like a college and simply have three terms with breaks in sensible places. It seems crazy to go nearly brain-dead during winter break only to return to school in time to kick it in gear for finals. What is with that anyway?

———

A couple of uneventful weeks pass and everyone seems quieter than usual around school. Maybe we're all just buckling down to our studies, or maybe it's simply the winter blahs. But to be fair, I can't blame my moodiness completely on finals. I can't even blame it on the cold, foggy weather, which really is depressing. The truth is, something else is bugging me. At first I tried to pretend it was no big deal. But as days pass and nothing changes, it begins to get to me. Now I'm getting concerned.

No, I'm not obsessing over a boy. I still like Conrad Stiles, and he seems to still like me. We've gone out a couple times since Christmas, but his schedule is pretty full with varsity basketball right now, which means I don't see him that much. But that's not what's getting to me anyway. It's something much bigger than Conrad, something I can't really talk to anyone about. I haven't even told Olivia. In some ways I haven't fully admitted it to myself.

But here is the truth: I feel like I haven't heard a word from God in ages. No dreams, no visions, nothing out of the ordinary. Just peace and quiet. I know I should be grateful. But I'm not.

Naturally, I read my Bible and pray regularly. How could I not? And, of course, I go to church and youth group, and while I get something out of all those things, I'm just not getting any special messages like I did before. As much as I hate to admit it, this has me seriously worried.

I haven't forgotten my little prayer on Christmas Eve, after the terrorist incident on the flight home from Phoenix. I was feeling weary. I remember how I begged God to give me a break.

And I think I might've sounded horribly ungrateful, like I was whining and complaining because God had used me to do something that really was amazing and miraculous. And now I wonder if He's decided to give that incredible gift to someone else. Someone more worthy. And by mid-January, right before finals week, I am feeling totally bummed. *What have I done?*

"Dear God," I pray before going to bed, "please, forgive me if I seemed unappreciative a few weeks ago. I really am glad that You chose me for that particular gift. I love thinking that You trust me enough to show me important things. I think I was just worn out from everything that had happened. I'm so sorry if I said or did something wrong. Please, forgive me for being so selfish. And if You want to give this gift back to me, I'll try to always be grateful for it. And I'll try to always use it for Your glory."

I take a deep breath and steady myself for this next line. "And, dear God, if You should choose not to give me this gift again, well, I just want You to know that it won't change how I feel about You. I will still love You and trust You—with all of my heart. Heavenly Father, I know You know what's best for me. I am Your servant. Amen."

Then I feel surprisingly peaceful as I go to sleep. And I suspect I might even have a dream tonight. But morning comes and, with it, no dream. At least nothing I can remember. Nothing that came from God. Just the same, I remember my promise to accept whatever God chooses for me. Even if that means it's over and He's not going to send me any more messages. I am okay with that.

Still, I try not to feel too disappointed as Olivia drives us to school that morning. I attempt to carry on what seems a normal conversation and don't tell her how I'm really feeling underneath. I ask about her three-day weekend. (It was Martin Luther King Day yesterday, and her dad took them skiing for all three days.)

"How was the snow?"

"Awesome. I wish you could've come, Sam."

"Me too," I admit. But I don't admit that the real reason I passed on the invitation was because of finances. I know Olivia would've offered to pay my way. But I also know that she does that too much. And as Mom likes to remind me, I need to accept that our family's finances are not the same as the Marsh family's. And while I try to save when I can, it seems that I'm usually pretty broke. Maybe I really should look for a serious part-time job.

"Good luck on your finals," I tell Olivia as we part ways to go to class.

Then I try to devote my full concentration to my finals. For the next couple of days, I try to block out the fact that God seems to be blocking me out. Okay, I know that's not true or even fair. But it's how it feels.

Maybe I should get used to it. Maybe this is simply the way it's going to be. I'll have a "normal" life and live the way other people do—trusting and serving God whether or not He communicates to me through supernatural means. Okay, fine. I can do that. I'm sure there've been times when that's all I wanted to do, times when the pressure of hearing God felt overwhelming. So why not just get used to this?

Finals week passes, and on Friday (a teachers' work-day) I'm considering getting some sort of job. I pray about this but don't feel any strong inclination one way or another. I've asked Mom's opinion, and naturally, she thinks it's a great idea.

"Unfortunately, we're cutting back due to budget prob-lems at the park district," she tells me. "Or else I'd suggest you try there. But even the day-care center is overstaffed right now."

The truth is, I'd rather work someplace where Mom doesn't anyway. I mean, I've always liked working with the kids there, and I might even consider applying for some-thing similar to that somewhere else. But it would be cool not to work where my mom is everyone's boss.

So I'm perusing the rather skimpy employment sec-tion of the classifieds, realizing that January isn't exactly the best time to be looking for part-time work. I jump when my cell phone rings, probably because it so seldom does these days. But that's mostly because I use it primarily for things related to Ebony and the local police department, although Olivia occasionally calls me on it when she can't get me on the landline. This morning Ebony's on the other end. I'm surprised at how happy I am to hear her voice.

"How's it going?" she asks in an offhanded manner.

"Okay. How about you?"

"I'm doing well. Had a nice break over the holidays. Now I'm back at work, and things are fairly quiet here."

"I guess that's good, huh?"

"In some ways, it is."

I can't think of anything to say now. And despite being glad to hear from her, I suddenly almost feel like crying.

"Well, I hadn't heard from you in a while, Samantha, and I sort of wondered if anything new is developing for you. Anything you want to talk about..."

It sounds like she's fishing, like she thinks I've been having some incredible crime-solving dreams and have been holding back on her. Yeah, right.

I force a pathetic laugh. "Nothing new here. Just finished finals week, and it's a no-school day. The truth is, I'm just sitting around in my pj's reading the paper."

"And you're really doing okay, Samantha?"

"I guess so..."

"You sound a little down."

"Well, I suppose I'm kinda worried about something." ·

"Want to talk?"

Do I want to talk? I'm not sure. What would I even say?

"Hey, got any plans for lunch?"

I sort of laugh. "Not really."

"How about if I take you to Rosie's?"

"Sounds good."

"Great. There's something I want to discuss with you."

"Cool."

A couple hours later, we're sitting at Rosie's, our lunch is history, and Ebony is telling me about a cold case she's working on. Apparently there has been a renewed interest in a young man who died from a gunshot wound to the head several years ago.

"His name was Peter Clark," she tells me. "At the time it seemed pretty cut-and-dried. Everyone assumed it was a suicide—there was a note and the wound appeared self-inflicted. But some new evidence has surfaced that suggests possible foul play." Then she goes on to tell me that Peter's mother suspects that someone murdered her son. And while this is kind of interesting in a very sad way, I'm confused.

"I'm not sure why you're telling me this," I finally say.

She looks uncomfortable now. "Well, I was hoping you might be able to help us."

"How?"

"Well, I thought if you looked at some photos and things...maybe you'd get a message from—"

"Ebony," I say a bit harshly, "you know that I'm not a medium. I don't connect with the dead and hear their—"

"I know," she says quickly. "But I thought if you were thinking about this boy, his circumstances and every-thing, maybe God would want to use you—to show you something."

"Usually the dreams and visions come as God gives them," I point out, thinking that maybe I should be speak-ing in the past tense since God hasn't given any for weeks now. "I can't just force them to come."

She nods. "I know… I shouldn't have asked."

Now I feel mean, like I've hurt her feelings. And then I think of all she's done for me, and I feel guilty.

"I'm sorry," I say. "To be honest, I don't really know how this gift works. I guess I shouldn't be so quick to say that God couldn't help me if I looked at some photos or things." I force a smile. "Anyway, it's probably worth a try."

Ebony looks relieved. "It's not like we can force God's hand."

I consider telling her my worries about God having removed His hand, but then maybe this is a turning point. Maybe God brought me to Ebony's mind because He is up to something. Anyway, I hope so!

Three

As Ebony drives us to the police station, I am unexpectedly excited, sort of like something good is about to happen to me. And okay, I'm torn because I also feel really guilty for feeling like this. I mean, how can I be happy about the prospect of learning more about some guy's death? Whether it was suicide or murder or whatever, it's still extremely sad, and there must be a family somewhere that is probably still mourning the loss of their loved one. Not unlike how I feel when I consider how my own dad was murdered while working on the police force about five years ago.

And so, as Ebony parks in the employee parking area, I decide I'm definitely *not* happy about this. I'm simply enthusiastic over the prospect of being used by God again, to think that I might be a tool in the possible resolution of what could turn out to be a murder case.

I really want to make myself totally available to God today. I pray silently as we walk up to the back door of city hall. Once again, I tell God that I'm here for Him. I'm ready and available for whatever He'd like me to do. I ask Him to help me tune in to His heart and His Spirit and to use me however He sees fit.

Ebony leads me downstairs to the crime lab, and soon we are looking through a cardboard box of "clues." Even though things are sealed in Ziploc bags, I have this very eerie feeling as I stare at them. To be honest, I feel like an intruder, like a voyeur who's peeking into private things, at personal items that I have no right to view.

"Are you sure this is okay?" I ask Ebony, my voice shaking just slightly.

"As long as *you're* okay."

I pick up a plastic sealed package of what I'm guessing was once a pale blue hand towel, now stained mostly brownish-red with dried blood. And suddenly I feel sick to my stomach.

"I need some air," I tell Ebony. She follows me back out of the stuffy lab, and I lean against the wall and attempt to calm my insides.

"Are you all right, Samantha?" She puts a steadying hand on my shoulder.

I nod and take in a deep breath. "Maybe this isn't such a good idea."

"Maybe not. Evidence can be pretty grisly."

"I hate to be such a baby. I mean, I saw some gnarly things in my dreams and visions when God was leading us to find Kayla. But somehow seeing these *real* things, up close like that, the dried blood and all…well, it's a little overwhelming."

"Trust me, you shouldn't feel bad. I've seen grown men come unglued when looking at various pieces of evidence or at a crime scene. That old saying 'The bigger they are, the harder they fall,' is really true."

"I'm sorry."

"Don't be sorry..." She pushes her bangs away from her forehead. "How about photos? Do you think that would help?"

I give her an uncertain look as I imagine reviewing some gruesome crime scene photos of a dead kid on the floor. "I—uh—"

"I mean photos of Peter when he was still alive, Samantha."

"Oh. Well, sure."

Ebony gets me a glass of water, and we go up to her office, where Peter's file is already on her desk. She peruses through it and finally produces a couple of color photos. Just random shots, it seems. One by a lake and one in front of what I'm guessing was his parents' Christmas tree. Sad. Peter Clark was a nice-looking guy with straight dark brown hair and what appear to be blue eyes. Not movie star handsome, but not a loser either. He does have what seems a sincere smile, and it makes me sad to think this guy is dead.

"How old was he when he died?"

"Eighteen." She hands me another photo. This one looks like a senior picture. He's standing in front of a tree, arms casually folded across his chest, smiling like he doesn't have a care in the world. "He died just a few weeks before his graduation."

"That's so sad."

"His family agreed that he hadn't been himself the month or two before he died. His mother chalked it up to pregraduation stress. But we recently learned that he might have been dabbling in drugs as well."

"Too bad." I study that sincere smile. What is it that makes some kids gravitate toward drugs? If I only had this photo to go by, I would've guessed that this was a guy who knew better. But then I could've said the same thing about my own brother. You just never know.

"A suicide note was sent to the family by way of a website Peter belonged to. He prearranged to have the note sent through e-mail, if you can imagine that."

"E-mail? How impersonal. But wouldn't it have arrived *before* Peter killed himself? Why didn't the family do something to prevent it?"

"It was all set up by Peter through this suicide website so it would arrive *after* his death."

"A *suicide* website?"

Ebony nods. "I know it sounds bizarre, not to mention gruesome. But there are sites that actually assist those who want to end their own lives."

"*Assist* them?" I am stunned. "How?"

"Oh, by giving information, handling suicide notes through e-mail so that they're sent after the fact, as in Peter's case. It's all very carefully set up, everything you need to know to check out." Ebony makes a disgusted sigh. "This wonderful age of information just keeps getting scarier and scarier."

"I guess." I hand her back the photo. What am I doing here? Why do I think I can possibly assist Ebony with

solving this crime? Well, if it was a crime, which is beginning to sound more and more unlikely.

"Sorry to sound so hopeless," she says. "But sometimes I just get angry."

"I understand. But like I keep telling you and everyone, I'm
not a medium, Ebony. I'm really not sure how I can help..."

"I know. I just thought it couldn't hurt to try."

"And like you know, God works in His own ways...His
own timing. I don't control Him or His messages." I want to
add, "And lately He doesn't seem to be speaking to me
anyway," but I don't. I can't bear to say those words.

"I realize that. But He also tells us to ask Him. The
Bible says *we have not because we ask not*. So I thought
I'd just ask." She smiles. "Can't hurt, can it?"

"I guess not. But still, I don't totally get this. Why is
Peter's case suddenly being reopened? It sounds like a
clear-cut suicide to me."

"It did to everyone else too. Back when it happened.
But now we've learned some things that cast a shadow of
doubt over it. Consequently, we promised the mother we'd
look into it again."

"What kinds of things?"

"Well, for one thing, there's that bit about drugs. No
one even suspected that Peter was involved with drugs."

"But couldn't that explain why he killed himself?"

"Definitely. But according to his mom, there's something about Peter's good friend Brett Carnes that doesn't
quite add up."

"What's that?"

"Well, it turns out he was involved in drugs too."

"Big surprise there."

"Yes, I know. But apparently he continues to be quite heavily involved—it seems he's actually been selling meth, for years now according to our source."

"Who's your source?"

"Peter's old girlfriend, Faith Mitchell."

"Oh."

"She e-mailed Peter's family around Christmas, coming forward with some information that could change everything."

"What made her come forward?"

"I guess she was into drugs too. According to Faith's note—it was sort of a confessional—she got hooked before Peter ever tried anything. Brett was her supplier. Faith had felt guilty for years, assuming she was the reason Peter gave in and tried drugs and eventually killed himself."

"That sounds reasonable."

"But it seems she changed her thinking. In her letter, she said that she wasn't really certain that Peter had actually used at all, claiming they'd never done it together, and she'd never seen him do it. Brett had told her Peter was using, and she simply believed him."

"Where's this Brett dude now?"

"We're not sure. Last we could track him, he was living in a small town in eastern Oregon, but he's not there now."

"So how do you know that Faith is reliable? I mean why, after all these years, has she suddenly decided to tell Peter's parents this?"

"In her letter, Faith said she'd gone through rehab and has been clean for several years now. She recently got married and is expecting their first child. She wanted to leave all this behind her, but it seems her conscience got to her. That's why she e-mailed Peter's parents telling them that she had a strong feeling Peter didn't kill himself. She said she couldn't prove anything, but she felt sure that Brett Carnes was involved somehow."

"Wow, that's quite an accusation."

Ebony nodded. "And quite difficult to prove."

"Where is Faith living now?"

"We don't know. She wants to remain anonymous. Even the e-mail was sent from an address that no longer exists."

"Well, if what she's saying is true, you can't blame her," I point out. "I mean, if I was involved with something that gnarly then cleaned up my act and was living a decent life, I'd want to leave it all behind too."

"Plus, being pregnant, she might be concerned for her safety if Peter's death really was a murder."

I sigh and shake my head. "Poor Faith."

"So, we really don't have much to go on," says Ebony. "Peter's untimely death, with physical evidence that all points to a self-inflicted gunshot wound. Faith's mysterious e-mail. A missing friend with a reputation in this town for dealing drugs. And the big question—did Peter really kill himself? Or was foul play involved?"

"But you mentioned that suicide website. Why would Peter get caught up in something like that unless he was really looking for a way out? And what about the suicide note?"

She nods. "Yes, lots of questions...not many answers."

"Do you think it's possible Faith has an ax to grind with Brett, that she might've written the e-mail hoping to get him in trouble?"

"The thought occurred to me. But according to what we can find, Faith Mitchell left town shortly after Peter's death. Brett didn't. In fact, he remained involved with the Clark family. He even befriended Peter's younger brother, Cody. Plus if Faith's still in contact with Brett and wants to get him in trouble, why wouldn't she give Peter's parents information regarding Brett's whereabouts?"

"I suppose you're right."

"Would you be willing to come out to Peter's house with me this afternoon?"

I shrug. "Okay. But, like I said, I'm not sure it'll do any good."

"I know. And it's not that I expect anything. But I'm just doing the asking thing. After hitting nothing but dead-ends, I've been asking God to show me the answers. And naturally, that made me think of you."

———

Peter's family's house is in a slightly run-down neighborhood of older homes. Mostly split-levels with yards that could use some TLC. Not impressive. I wait as Ebony knocks on a beat-up door in need of paint. In fact, the whole house looks like it has seen better days. Or maybe it's just sad. A worn-out-looking middle-aged woman with mousy brown hair answers the door, and when she sees that it's Ebony, a trace of hope flickers across her faded blue eyes.

"Have you discovered something new?" she asks.

"We're still working on it," Ebony assures her, introducing me. "Samantha has helped me on other unusual cases. She has a gift for things like this."

Mrs. Clark looks curious, but thankfully doesn't press me with questions. "I just want to find out the truth," she says to me. "I feel like I can't rest until I know what really happened—why it happened."

"I understand."

"Samantha's father died tragically too," says Ebony. "She knows what it's like to lose someone dear."

Mrs. Clark pats my arm. "I'm sorry for your loss."

"I hope I can be of help," I say, feeling totally helpless.

"Do you mind if we go down to the basement?" asks Ebony.

"Go right ahead." Mrs. Clark nods toward a door near the kitchen. "But I won't go down there...I can't."

"That's okay," says Ebony. "I don't blame you."

A preteen boy looks up from where he's using a PlayStation that's connected to the TV in the family room. "Are you the policewoman?" he asks Ebony in a flat-sounding voice that doesn't seem to match his inquisitive blue eyes.

"I am."

"This is Cody," says Mrs. Clark. "Peter's younger brother. There's no school today."

We introduce ourselves, and I can't help but ask about the game he's playing since it's the same one my brother,

Zach, used to play—until Mom discovered how violent it was and banned it from our home. "Is that *Killer7*?"

He looks somewhat surprised, then nods. "Do you play it too?"

"It's too violent for me," I say, hoping his mom will take a hint. I can't believe she lets this kid play a game that's all about murder and killing, especially in light of his brother's tragic death. But despite my comment, she seems totally oblivious.

As we go down the steep wooden stairs to the basement, Ebony tells me that Peter died down here. "I'm surprised his family continued living here," she says in a hushed tone, although I'm sure Mrs. Clark can't hear us. "But I suppose Mrs. Clark had no choice since their marriage broke up shortly after Peter's death. Suicide can be hard on everyone."

"They got divorced because of Peter?"

"I don't know all the details. I just know that when someone takes his own life, everyone tends to feel guilty."

I remember how guilt ridden I was when my dad died. I blamed myself for not believing the dream God had given me—for not warning Dad—not that it would have changed anything. Still, it took me years to get over it. So, in a way, I can understand how the Clarks might be feeling now. So sad.

I look around a frumpy room, which has bad wood paneling and a really pathetic plaid couch. "This kind of reminds me of *That 70s Show*," I tell her. "Only in a Stephen King sort of way."

"I know what you mean." Ebony goes over and stands next to a coffee table that has fake wagon wheels for legs. "But Peter and his friends liked hanging down here. There used to be an old TV and VCR over in that corner. But I guess they moved that out." She looks around. "Everything else is pretty much the same."

I slowly walk around the room, hoping for something— I'm not sure what—but nothing happens. The room smells musty, as if it hasn't been opened in years. And it's cold— very cold. I'm glad I still have my coat on.

"He shot himself over here." Ebony stands in an open part of the room not far from the only small window, which is so encrusted with dust that it barely lets in light.

I nod without saying anything. What can you say? This is so depressing. All I want to do is get out of here. "I don't see how his mom and brother can stand living in this house," I suddenly say as I turn away. "It seriously creeps me out. And why she lets him play that awful video game..."

"I feel the same way," Ebony says in a sad voice. "But I thought it would be worth it to visit... I mean, if it helped at all."

I stand for a long moment, eyes tightly closed, barely breathing, as I focus in on God, begging Him to show me something. Reminding Him of what Ebony said about "*Ask and you shall receive.*" But nothing happens. No answers come. Not even the tiniest speck of a vision. Just silence so thick that I can feel it pressing in on me from all sides. Why won't God talk to me? Have I angered Him? Offended Him?

And suddenly I begin to cry. Not just quietly either. I am sobbing.

Four

I—I'm not going to—to be any help to you," I choke out the words, embarrassed by the uncontrollable tears now streaming down my cheeks as I stand across from the grimy window where Peter supposedly took his life.

"Oh, Samantha." Ebony comes over and puts her arms around me and gently pats my back as I continue to cry. After a while, she tells me that she's sorry and that she shouldn't have brought me here. "I'm probably just try-ing too hard."

"No, it's not your fault." I step back and wipe my wet face with the backs of my hands. "It's just—just that God isn't talking to me anymore," I blurt out. "He hasn't given me a dream or a vision or anything. Not since—since I told Him to give me a break."

Ebony looks like she's about to laugh. *"You told God to give you a break?"*

I nod, swallowing hard to hold back my tears. "After we got back from Phoenix, I told God I was tired. I asked Him to leave me alone and give me a break."

Now she actually does laugh. "Well, you *needed* a break, girlfriend! You'd been strung pretty thin over the whole Kayla affair. And God certainly used you in a big way down there, and then we had that terrorist business on the flight home. Good grief, who could blame you for wanting a break?"

"But I shouldn't have said those things to God. I sounded so ungrateful and whiney and—"

"Oh, Samantha, do you really think you could possibly offend God? Do you think you could stop God from doing what He wants to do?"

I just shrug.

"Don't you remember Jonah? How he tried to ditch God by hopping on a slow boat to China, or something to that effect? But God never left that man alone. *Remember*?"

"Yeah." I replay the old story through my head. The reluctant prophet who didn't want to tell the people God's warnings and how God didn't let him off the hook, so to speak. Then even after being swallowed and barfed up by a whale, Jonah still tried to ignore God. But eventually Jonah had to listen—and obey.

"So, can't you see? If God wants to give you a vision or dream, *He will*. He's not going to let something you said stop Him, Samantha. He's a whole lot bigger than that."

I sort of laugh. "Now that you put it that way, I do sound pretty silly, huh?"

"So, just lighten up. God is the Giver of the gift, and it's up to Him. Right?"

"You're right."

"Now let's get out of here."

Mrs. Clark is expectantly waiting upstairs. I can see that she is desperate for us to tell her something, anything—like a starving dog waiting for a tiny morsel—the smallest bit to help her through her agony. I actually shoot up a silent prayer, begging God to give me something that will bring comfort.

"Would you like to see pictures of Peter?" she eagerly asks us, almost as if she's afraid to let us go quite yet.

"Sure," I say, although I would rather not. His story is so sad. I just want to get out of here and away from it.

Then she leads us past where Cody is still glued to his game and shooting people with all sorts of weapons, taking us over to the brick fireplace, where some cheaply framed photos of Peter and his soccer team are arranged on the wooden mantel. I look at Peter with his trombone, Peter holding up his little brother when Cody was still small.

"He was a nice-looking guy," I say for lack of anything better.

"He was a good boy too," she says in a slightly defensive tone. "I don't care what others say. He *was* a good boy."

"I'm really asking God to show us something," I tell her. "I believe that He is the one with all the answers, and I'm asking Him to give some to us."

She peers at me. "Are you a Christian?"

I nod. "I am."

She frowns. "I used to go to church back when the children were small, but I don't have much use for God anymore. Not after all this. What kind of a God lets these things happen?"

"I know how you feel," I say. "I felt the same way after my dad was murdered."

She looks slightly surprised by my confession.

"But I finally got to the place where I decided that I would rather be unhappy *with* God than unhappy *without* Him." I smile at her. "After that, I discovered that God is the only one who could make me happy again anyway. So it was sort of a win-win situation."

She shakes her head. "I'm afraid you have more faith than me."

"Faith is a gift," I tell her, knowing this is true but fearing it sounds a little trite. "God is the One who gives us faith."

She just looks at me with those sad, empty eyes. She is not buying it.

Then Ebony makes a move for the door. "Well, thanks for letting us look around, and you take care, Mrs. Clark. I'll be sure to let you know if I find out anything new."

"Yes, please do," calls Mrs. Clark. "Anything at all."

––––––––

"I appreciate you coming with me today," Ebony says as she pulls into my driveway. "And I'm sorry if it was upsetting."

"No, I'm okay. The hardest part was about how I'm not hearing from God lately. But just telling you...and what you said... Well, I do feel better now. Thanks."

"And I know you'll let me know if God does give you some information regarding Peter or any of that."

"Definitely." Although I doubt that's going to happen. Still, I don't mention this to her as I wave good-bye and go into the house.

The phone is ringing when I get inside. I answer it just in time to catch Olivia on the other end.

"Hey, I was about to give up," she says. "Where've you been all day?"

So without going into all the gory details, I tell her a little about my attempt to help Ebony with her cold case.

"Sounds kinda sad and interesting. Do you think God will show you something?"

"I have absolutely no idea," I admit in a glum voice. "In some ways I feel more in the dark about my little 'gift' than ever."

"It's kind of ironic, Sam."

"What?"

"Well, I can recall a few times when you were so frustrated that you hoped you'd *never* have another dream or vision. You felt it was too much responsibility. Remember?"

I consider this. "Yeah, but then it got to be sort of exciting too."

She laughs. "I know."

"Okay, just call me fickle. And obviously, God's calling the shots anyway. I guess He probably wants me to do some waiting—maybe He's working on my patience."

"Well, while you're patiently waiting, do you want to go to the basketball game tonight? Maybe it'll cheer you up to cheer for Conrad."

"Sounds good." So we arrange for her to pick me up in time to grab something to eat before the game.

The game is really exciting, but our team ends up losing in the last few seconds, which I know will bum Conrad, and consequently we don't stick around to wait for the team to come out of the locker room.

Olivia asks if I want to get coffee or something afterward, but I'm feeling kind of bummed too. I know it's only partly due to the game. The rest probably relates to what I've learned about Peter Clark today and my strong desire for God to show me something.

"You're being pretty quiet," Olivia says as we drive through the dark night.

"Sorry. I guess I'm still stuck on why God doesn't want to show me something in regard to Peter."

"It hasn't even been twenty-four hours," Olivia points out.

"I know. But I just get this feeling it's not coming. Like the door is closed and I can't open it."

"God's door," she says. "Guess He can close it if He wants, huh?"

"But I was thinking about other sorts of gifts, Olivia. I mean, if someone has the gift of teaching, they pretty much teach at will, don't they? Or the gift of encouragement? They just open their mouths and encourage others whenever others need it, right?"

"I suppose."

"And yet those are gifts, right?"

"Yeah."

"So, why is my gift different?"

"Maybe because it's a special gift, Sam. Like it needs some restrictions. Maybe God doesn't want you going overboard with it. I mean think about it—if you thought you could just close your eyes and suddenly have important knowledge about things that no one else has, well, don't you think that could get a little dangerous?"

I think about this and realize she's right. "Yeah, I guess so."

"Not to change the subject, but someone's having a birthday next week."

I perk up a little. "Yeah, as a matter of fact, someone is."

"Any big plans?"

I roll my eyes. "Yeah, right. Mom's so busy, as usual, that I haven't even dropped her any hints this year. I wouldn't be surprised if she totally forgets."

"Poor Samantha."

I laugh. "Thanks for the pity."

"Well, I'll try to think of some way we can celebrate. Even if it's just you and me, okay?"

"Sounds good to me."

"So keep that night open. It's on Saturday, isn't it?"

"Yeah." Then she pulls up at my house, and I thank her for the ride and go inside. It looks like my mom finally got home from work, but since the house is pretty quiet, I'm guessing she's gone to bed already and it's not even ten yet.

I walk around the semi-dark house for a while, just quietly going in and out of the rooms like I'm looking for something, although I don't know what it could possibly be. If anyone were watching me, they'd probably wonder about my state of mind. Maybe I wonder too. But sometimes I do this.

At first it's sort of comforting to wander around the house and remember things we did here together as a family. I remember how my dad and Zach would sit there on the couch and play Zach's latest video game—never anything as lethal as *Killer7*—at least while dad was alive. I also remember how sometimes all four of us would make popcorn and watch a video together, usually some G-rated Disney flick since Mom didn't approve of Zach and me being exposed to violence or questionable content of any kind when we were young. This still strikes me as strangely ironic considering how my dad was murdered in the line of duty. I guess parents can't protect you from everything.

I don't know exactly why, but I am suddenly feeling really, really lonely. And sad. And I wonder why our family has turned out the way it has. I mean, with Dad gone, never to come back again. And now Zach's gone too. Oh, I realize he'll probably be back someday and hopefully in a lot better shape than when he left. But it's like the McGregors have been torn apart. Like we've been broken and we can't quite get fixed again.

I think my sense of hopelessness is partly due to my mom turning her back on God. Oh, she doesn't use those words. She just says she's too busy or not interested. But I know that underneath she's mad at God. The same way I used to be. The way Mrs. Clark was today. And sometimes I try to talk to her about it, but she just shuts down and sometimes even gets mad. I don't remember my mom getting mad so much when we were kids, back when my dad was around to sort of buffer things and take up the slack. But in the past few years it seems like little things can easily set her off. And so, in a way, I should be glad that she's gone to bed. But just the same, I'm still lonely.

Eventually the house feels too big for me, and I go up to my room, turn on the lights, put in a quiet CD, and close my door. I wish I'd said yes when Olivia mentioned the idea of me spending the night at her house tonight. But at the time I felt tired and thought I just wanted to go home. Now I wish I wasn't here.

"Time to plug in to God," I tell myself out loud. Then I open my Bible and begin to read. And then I pray. After that, I write some things in my journal. And by the time I'm done, I feel a lot better. Okay, I'm not exactly jubilant, but I'm fine. And as it turns out, I actually am pretty tired and relieved to sleep in my own bed.

When I wake up in the morning, it feels like I'm on the cusp of a dream. And although I can't be sure, it seems like a special dream. I force my sleepy mind to try to remember, and then it all comes back. I was dreaming about my dad. It was my birthday and he had given me a gift in a big box with silver paper and a pale blue bow. I couldn't wait to open it, and it took a long time. There were layers and layers of paper, and as I peeled off still another sheet of gift wrap, the anticipation kept increasing. Then finally I got it off and opened the big box, and the only thing in there was a little brown plastic horse, the kind that comes from a cheap package of assorted farm animals. I held up the horse and yelled at my dad. "Why did you give me this stupid thing?" I shrieked again and again.

I was so furious and out of control that I feel embarrassed just to remember it now; then I remind myself it was just a dream. Not real. Not even from God. *Get over it, Sam.*

Even so, I keep thinking about the dream as I go into the kitchen, like my mind's stuck on a track and can't get off. Mom has already made coffee and I'm guessing has already gone to work as well since it's after nine. I pour myself a cup of slightly stale-smelling coffee, add some milk to tone down the acidity, and continue to ruminate over what the significance of Dad giving me a plastic horse might be. Why was I so rude and ungrateful to my dad? Why did I keep getting madder and madder just because he hadn't given me what I wanted? Although, to be fair, I don't even know what it was I wanted. Still, I was throwing the worst temper tantrum.

As I put the milk carton back in the fridge I flash back to my seventh birthday (ten years ago) and how all I wanted was a bike. A very specific bike. My neighbor Jennie, who has long since moved, had what I thought was the perfect bicycle. A pink and purple Barbie bike with all the cool accessories, including a white plastic wicker basket with pink and purple plastic daisies. But even after making my request clearly known to "Santa," I had been severely disappointed not to get my dream bike for Christmas. Consequently I spent the next few weeks dropping not-so-subtle hints and praying unceasingly for a Barbie bike to arrive on my birthday. And the night before the big morning, I felt sure there was a buzz in the air and

was certain it had to do with me and a certain Barbie bike
that I would find parked in the living room the next morning.
Maybe with a big pink bow on it.

I was so excited I almost couldn't sleep. And when I
got up the next morning, there really was a bicycle parked
in the living room. And it had a bow on it; I don't recall
what color now. But this bike was *not* a Barbie bike!
Instead of the coveted Barbie bike, this one was a light
blue girls' Schwinn.

I didn't know what to do, and while having a bike of
my own was nice, I was *not* a happy camper. In fact,
I was pretty upset. Of course, I was only seven at the
time, but I had never felt so conflicted about anything in
my entire life. On one hand, it was a decent bike and my
parents were trying and I should've been grateful. But on
the other hand, I had made my desires crystal clear—*why
wasn't it the Barbie bike?*

I can't remember what I did exactly, or maybe my
memory is giving me a break, but somehow my extreme
disappointment was communicated (I think I probably cried
a lot). And later that day I overheard Mom and Dad discussing my little dilemma. Mom was telling him that he
should've gotten me the Barbie bike like I wanted, and
Dad was saying that he knew I'd outgrow it and be sorry
to own such a "sissy cycle." I'm pretty sure that's what he
called it too.

It took me a while to get over the whole thing, but in
the long run, Dad's reasoning turned out to be right on.
I still remember the day, just a couple years later, when I

was riding bikes with Jennie. We stopped at the park, where some fourth grade boys began to tease Jennie mercilessly. *"Where'd you get the baby Barbie bike?"* they taunted, along with other things. And although I felt sorry for my friend, I also remember holding my head high as we pedaled away, she on her sissy cycle and me on my suddenly sophisticated Schwinn.

I take a sip of my coffee. So Dad really did know best. Of course, I couldn't see that when I was seven. Yet, on the same note, I feel sure that God, the Giver of gifts, knows best too.

Five

The next week passes quietly. Quietly, as in God's not saying anything to me. But I keep thinking about Peter Clark and wondering what really happened to him. Or is it simply as it appears? I've even gone online and read some old news stories about his death, which hasn't been terribly informative or helpful. Peter used his dad's handgun, which his dad kept in the nightstand in the master bedroom. Nothing was locked up, and both boys knew it was there. Why do parents do that? Not all parents, of course. My dad, being a cop, never would've done something that lame. Anyway, according to what I read, all the forensics evidence and fingerprints indicated nothing more than a suicide, and then the e-mailed note seemed to seal the deal. End of story. Or not.

I'm just not sure and it's bugging me. Did Peter really kill himself? Or was something else going on with that friend Brett? And was Peter really experimenting with drugs? Or was that just a contrived story? And if so, why?

Naturally, I have absolutely no idea. And I don't even know why I bother to think about this whole sad thing, except that I feel so badly for his family. But I have been praying for his mom and brother—a lot. Unfortunately,

I don't think there's much more I can do. And like I told Ebony when she called to check on me yesterday, I don't have a single thing on it. And I suspect I just need to let it go. Move on.

We've started the new quarter, which means a few new classes, including chemistry, which I'm sure is a big mistake on my part, although I managed to snag the smartest kid in the class for my lab partner. Garrett Pierson is a shy, sort of nerdish guy who seems to be into all things science-related. Consequently, he's already taken the lead on our first project, which I don't totally understand, something to do with energy. Not that I plan to slack exactly. But it's reassuring to know that my grade is in good hands, specifically Garrett's.

For the most part, school has felt pretty boring and tedious this week, and I think everyone's in the doldrums of winter right now. Plus the weather is cold and wet and cruddy. But at least I have a birthday coming up on Saturday. Not that I have any great expectations, although Olivia has been somewhat mysterious and I think she might be up to something. Most of all I think it'll be fun to be seventeen. For some reason, seventeen sounds a lot more sophisticated and grown-up than sixteen. Nearly eighteen…adulthood just around the corner.

"Coming to the game tonight?" Conrad asks me after lunch on Friday.

"You guys going to win this one?" I tease.

"We're playing Fairview," he says, as in "duh" and it should be obvious. Everyone knows that Fairview High isn't known for its athletics.

"Then you guys better win," I tell him. "Guess I'll come."

"If you stick around afterward, we could go get some pizza," he offers. "Maybe Alex and Olivia would want to come along too."

"I'll ask Olivia."

"Where you headed?"

I groan. "Chemistry."

He nods. "Oh, yeah, I forgot you were taking that. You're a brave woman."

"Don't you mean stupid?"

He laughs. "Well, I didn't want to say that. You won't catch me taking one of Dynell's classes. He's tough; I've heard it's a sure way to mess up your GPA."

"I just wanted to finish up my science credits this year. That way I can take it easier for senior year."

"But chemistry?" He makes a face.

"Like I told you, it's all there was to choose from."

Garrett Pierson hurries past us, his head held down like usual, like maybe he's counting the cracks in the side-walk, although it's not a sidewalk and there are no cracks. It's simply the gray industrial carpeted hallway that leads to the science department.

"And besides," I say in a lowered voice, nodding to the hunched back of my slightly geekish chemistry cohort, "I've got a good partner to get me through."

"Garrett Pierson?"

"That's right. He's really smart."

"Should I be jealous?"

I turn and look at Conrad, and even if his curly red hair is a little goofy, he's ten times better looking than poor Garrett. "Yeah, right."

He grins and gives me a peck on the cheek, something I'm still not quite comfortable with at school, then says, "See ya," and heads off toward his class. I guess everyone probably thinks of us as a couple now, but I still don't feel totally sure myself. Not that Conrad is seeing anyone else, but I suppose I'm just not used to this exclusive thing yet. And I don't think I'll ever use the term "going steady" because it sounds so stupid.

Of course, Olivia thinks it's great that Conrad and I are "dating," and she wishes that she and Conrad's friend Alex were a couple. But so far they mostly do things with us, as a foursome, and it hasn't gotten very serious between them.

Olivia's worried that Alex might have his eye on Brittany Fallows, which I think is ridiculous. I mean, those two might've gone together back in middle school, but I've heard Brittany putting Alex down and I seriously doubt they'll ever get back together again. Olivia just needs to chill. Maybe act a little less interested. Guys don't like being chased.

"Of course, I'm in," Olivia tells me when I pass Conrad's invitation for her and Alex to join us after the game tonight. "I'll pick you up sevenish, and we can watch the end of the JV game before varsity plays." She sounds happy as she chatters all the way home from school. I think she's feeling hopeful about Alex, and I want to warn her to go easy tonight, but I don't want to be a downer.

The house feels icy cold when I get home. I know Mom is trying to save on the gas bill by turning the heat off during the day. Trying to ignore the damp chill in the air, I fix myself a cup of cocoa and keep my jacket on for a while. But then I think, *This is ridiculous. Why am I freezing in my own home?*

That's when I decide to start a fire in the fireplace. It's something my dad used to do on a cold winter's day, but something we rarely do anymore. Mom and I didn't even have a fire in there at Christmas. But suddenly I wonder why not. I mean, we still have lots of firewood. Sure it's a little work, but maybe it'll cheer this place up.

So I gather newspaper and kindling and get everything all ready to go, just like Dad used to do; then I use one of those long matches and light it up. Unfortunately, I didn't think to open the flue first. The next thing I know, smoke is going everywhere, and before long the smoke alarm in the kitchen is blaring, and I don't know what to do.

I used a lot of newspaper, and the flames are so hot that I can't put my hand in to open it up. I run around the smoky house with the obnoxious alarm screaming like a wounded animal, until I finally decide to use an oven mitt and the fire poker. After several feeble attempts, I get the stupid thing open.

Of course, now the family room and kitchen are full of smoke. And I smell like smoke. But I manage to disarm the fire alarm and I open some windows, which makes it even colder in here. Then I turn on the exhaust fan over the stove and in the powder room, and after a while, it thins a bit, but it's still a little gray looking, and my eyes are burning. Naturally, as I'm trying to clean the air, my fire, which only had kindling on it, goes out for lack of wood. I would make a pathetic Boy Scout.

"What is going on here?" Mom demands as she walks in the front door. It figures that this would be an early day for her. It's not even five and here she is. Just great.

I try to explain what I've been doing, even trying to make it sound funny, but I can tell by the hardness in her eyes that she's angry. "It smells like you tried to burn the house down."

"I'm sorry, but it was cold in here."

"Then turn up the stupid thermostat."

"But sometimes you get mad when I turn it up," I point out, which is true. She's yelled at me twice this week for having it turned up too high, although it was barely over seventy.

"Well, then learn how to use the fireplace correctly before you go and burn the place to the ground!" She picks up the disarmed smoke alarm, which is still on the kitchen counter, its wires and batteries splayed about like it exploded, and thrusts it at me. "And put this thing back up!" Then she storms off to her room, and I want to scream. What right does she have to come in here and act like that? I mean, who's the adult here?

Grumbling to myself, I put the smoke alarm back together, climb on the kitchen stool, and reattach it to the holder on the ceiling. Suddenly, I cannot wait until I'm eighteen and old enough to move out of here and live on my own. Seriously, my mom can be unbearable sometimes. It's like she thinks she's the only one in the world with problems, like no one else in this family is hurting at all, like she's the center of the universe and it's all about her.

Sure, I know her life's not that great, but I also know that if she'd just come back to the Lord, things would get a whole lot better. And not just for her. I'm sure my life would improve if my mom would start living like a believer again. It'd probably even help Zach. But will she even consider this relatively simple solution? Not on your life. She can be so stubborn.

I walk past the smoldering ashes in the fireplace and am about to stomp up to my room and slam the door, just to send her a not-so-subtle message, but then I realize that I still want a fire. So I start all over again.

Okay, I suppose I might be doing this just to spite my mom. To show her that I do know what I'm doing and that I'm not, after all, a total idiot. Or maybe I just want a fire to get warm by. Who knows? Who cares? It's done. Before long, there's actually a nice cheerful fire snapping and crackling in the fireplace. So there!

I decide to get something to eat and to enjoy it by *my* fire. I know the mature thing to do would be to invite her to join me, but I'm still miffed. So I go ahead and make myself a nice grilled cheese sandwich, ignoring the fact that it would be easy to make my mom one too, and ignoring that the other half of the frying pan is empty. *Let her make her own sandwich if she wants one.* Chances are I'd make it for her and she'd turn her nose up at it anyway. She'd probably inform me that it was full of cholesterol. I make myself another mug of cocoa too.

So I sit on the hearth by my toasty fire, about to dig into my nice hot sandwich and cocoa when Mom comes down the stairs. She walks toward me then just stands between the kitchen and the family room and looks at me with this pitifully sad expression, like she doesn't have a friend in the world, including me, her only daughter. And suddenly I feel extremely guilty and greedy and incredibly immature—not to mention not a very nice Christian either. Good grief, why didn't I just make her a sandwich too?

"I would've made you one," I say, sheepishly holding up my golden brown sandwich. "But I didn't know if—"

"That's okay," she says in a sad voice. "I'll fix myself something."

"Sorry..."

Then she turns and goes into the kitchen. I hear her knocking around in there, and she drops something and lets out a swear word, and I feel even worse than before. Really, why am I so self-centered? Would it have hurt me to be a little more thoughtful?

I take a bite, but the sandwich tastes a little like sawdust now. And even though it will cool off, I decide to wait in case Mom wants to join me out here. She eventually does, but all she has is a bowl of some sad-looking canned soup that she obviously nuked in the microwave. Real appetizing.

"Nice fire," she murmurs as she sits on the couch across from me.

"Thanks." I take a bite of my now cold sandwich and chew.

"Sorry I yelled at you."

I nod. "And I'm sorry about the smoke and everything."

Then we both eat in silence, and despite the fire, it still feels cold in here. Just to have something to talk about, to lighten it up, I almost mention that it's my birthday tomorrow—in case she's forgotten, which seems a possibility. But as I open my mouth I see that her eyes are bright with tears. She looks like she's about to cry.

"Are you okay, Mom?"

She shakes her head as if she's unsure, but then sets her spoon down into her bowl with a clink and looks at me.

"Is something wrong at work?"

She shrugs, but the tears are coming now. "Just the usual stress. Budget cuts, having to lay people off, disgruntled employees, the norm for this time of year."

"I'm sorry…"

She pulls a tissue from her jacket pocket and wipes a tear.

"Is that why you're sad?" I persist, uncertain as to whether she really wants to talk about this or not. But knowing my mom, if she doesn't want to talk, no one can make her.

"I—I don't know…"

"Is it because of me? Because of the smoke and not making you a sandwich?"

She sort of smiles now, although it's a halfhearted smile. "No, Samantha, it's not because of you."

"Zach?" I say suddenly. "Have you heard anything about Zach that's—"

"No, I spoke to him on Wednesday. He sounded good. He thinks he'd like to stay in treatment longer, maybe even do the full ninety days."

"Oh, good." I study Mom and try to figure out what's making her blue. Is it really just work?

"Your dad always made fires..."

"Yeah."

"I guess this fire just made me think of him...remember things..."

"And that's why you're sad?"

She sighs deeply. "Maybe a little."

"Is it something more?"

"I guess I'm just lonely, Sam. It's been hitting me hard lately. Here I am in my forties, you kids are practically gone, and I just feel like I've been left behind—or I'm about to be. It's depressing."

I consider pointing out that I'll be around a while yet, that I have another year of high school, but I don't think that's going to help her at the moment. For some reason I think there's something else going on here. I think she's lonely in another way. "Why don't you start dating, Mom?"

She looks a little surprised. Then she laughs, but not in a happy way. "I'm afraid that's easier said than done."

"What do you mean?"

"I mean I don't even know any available single men that I'd care to go out with. And if I did, I wouldn't even be sure how to go about it. I think it would be hopeless."

"It's not hopeless. You just have to do it, Mom. It's not that hard."

"Maybe not for you. And just for the record, I had no problem dating when I was your age either. But things change."

"What kinds of things?"

"Well, for one thing, I don't have the kind of energy I used to have when I was younger. I work so much that by the time I get home I usually just want to crash."

I nod, but stop myself from saying, "I've noticed."

"And even if an interesting guy did come my way...well, I just don't have that much self-confidence anymore." She looks down at her somewhat dated gray pantsuit, similar to most of her other boring work clothes—functional and practical, but not very cute. "I feel as if I've lost my sense of style. Sometimes I don't even know who I am." She shakes her head. "I think I really might be hopeless."

"You're *not* hopeless, Mom. But I think you're like one of those women I saw on *Oprah* the other day. You've been so busy taking care of everything and everyone else that you've forgotten to take care of yourself.

"That sounds about right."

"But why can't that change?" I challenge her. "Why can't you take more time for yourself?"

"I don't know..."

"Why do you have to work so many hours anyway? It's not like they pay you extra for all the time you give them down there."

"That's true. But it's become a habit. When I took on the new position and started working full time, right after your dad died, well, I felt like I had to work extra hard just to prove myself."

"But haven't you done that by now? I mean, everyone down there really loves you, Mom. They all respect you. I've seen it when I'm there. Why can't you ease up a little?"

She actually seems to consider this. "I suppose I could try. This is the slow time of year anyway."

"Yeah," I say quickly, wanting to keep this thing going. "And if you weren't so busy, you could take some time to focus on yourself for a change, figure out who you are and what you need—what it'll take to make you happy." Of course, I want to add, "And you could start coming to church again," but I don't want to shut her down either. I feel like I'm making some headway, even if I'm not sure where we're going with it.

She almost smiles. "I don't even know where I'd begin, Samantha. The idea of focusing on myself, figuring out who I am, all that... Well, it's a bit overwhelming."

"Maybe you could start on your appearance," I say, then wish I hadn't since I can tell I've offended her.

"What would you suggest?" she asks in a stiff voice.

"Well, maybe you could change your hairstyle."

She runs her hand over her lifeless brown hair, which is streaked with gray and appears to be thinning. It's cut in the same style she's worn for years, a limp and boring bob with flat bangs. It only adds to the whole tired and worn-out look. "How would I change it?"

"I don't know. But I'm sure we could think of something. And maybe we could go shopping too. We could help get your wardrobe out of last millennium."

"Thanks a lot."

"It's true, Mom. You look totally out-of-date. And you're really not that old."

"According to whom?"

"Well, how about Bev Marsh?" I remind her of Olivia's mom. "She's older than you, but she dresses a lot more stylishly."

"She also has the money to do it."

"Hey, I manage to stay in style without spending as much as Olivia. You don't have to go broke to look good."

"Well, that might be, but I don't want to end up looking like a teenybopper either."

"You can look good without looking juvenile."

She stands up now and looks at the mirror that hangs over the fireplace mantel. "I suppose a little makeover wouldn't hurt, would it?"

"Not at all," I say with enthusiasm. "Want to start on it tomorrow?" Now, okay, it might be my birthday tomorrow, but this is important, and I could make a sacrifice. And who knows, it might be fun to help Mom get her act together.

"Not tomorrow," she says with reservation. "I really do have to go to work."

"When then?" I fold my arms across my chest. "You can't just put it off."

"How about next weekend? How about if I make sure that I'm not working? We'll go into Portland and do it up right. Make a whole day of it."

"It's a date."

"Good." She smiles. "Thanks, Sam."

"And speaking of dates, I should get ready. Olivia will be here soon to take me to the game, and we're doing pizza with Conrad and Alex afterward."

"Oh, to have a life..." she says wistfully.

"Well, I have a feeling all that's about to change for you, Mom. You might want to start getting yourself mentally prepared."

She sort of laughs, and then I dash up to my room to do a quick change and fix up before Olivia gets here.

Later that night, after our team wins the game, and after I've been hanging with my friends, eating pizza, and just basically acting like a kid and having a good time, I suddenly remember Mom and how sad she seemed earlier this evening. I consider how boring her life must be. Good grief, all she does is work and come home. No wonder she's grumpy so much of the time.

"Something wrong?" Conrad and I are walking across the parking lot after the employees at the pizza place threatened to lock us inside since they were closing for the night. Alex and Olivia already went home in her car, which she seemed pleased about, and it's just the two of us. "You got so quiet just now."

"Nothing's wrong," I tell him. "I'm fine. I was just thinking about my mom."

"How's she doing?"

So I explain a bit about how she's feeling lonely. "I think
she wants to start dating."

"Really?" He puts his arm around my shoulder and
gives me a squeeze. "Can't blame her for that."

"Yeah, but it's kind of weird too."

"You mean the idea of your mom going out?"

"Yeah. I mean, I've only seen her with Dad. And I suppose I sort of thought that was it. Dad's gone and now
Mom will be alone. End of story. I never really considered
what it would be like to have another guy in the picture."

"It'll probably take some getting used to."

"I guess."

"So, maybe you should be on the lookout for nice
older dudes." He opens the car door for me. "Like maybe
someone from church. You could set her up."

I laugh. "That'd be the day." But as Conrad drives me
home, I think maybe the boy is on to something. If I could
get Mom interested in a Christian guy, it might get her to
come back to church. By the time we get to my house,
I already have something of a plan in place.

I tell him what I'm plotting and ask him to help. "We
need to find a single guy who's fun and good-looking and
living for God and—"

"That's a tall order, Sam."

"Well, God can do it. Most of all, I guess we'll have to
be praying."

He firmly nods. "That I can do." Then he kisses me good night, and for a blissful moment I forget all about Mom and everything else.

"See ya tomorrow."

"Huh?" I say, wondering if he has something specific in mind since it's Saturday and he hasn't asked me out.

He grins. "You know, whatever. See ya!"

SIX

On Saturday morning I sleep in, as usual, and when I get up Mom has already gone to work, as usual. I look around the kitchen thinking maybe she's left a birthday card or something to show that she knows what day it is. But it seems she has forgotten. I'm not too surprised. Disappointed, yes, but I sort of figured she has a lot on her mind and is too busy to remember something as insignificant as her only daughter's seventeenth birthday. Okay, it sounds like I'm about to start having a pity party, and I'm not. I refuse to give in to it today.

Still, so much for celebrating my big day on the home front. It's sure not like it used to be when we were kids growing up. I remember how Dad usually made a special breakfast on birthdays, and there would be cards and gifts and balloons and hugs. This makes me wonder if Zach might actually remember my birthday, but then I doubt it. He's probably preoccupied now, and he's never been good at things like that in the first place. I almost always have to remind him of Mom's birthday and Mother's Day and things like that. I refuse to remind him of my birthday. After all, I'm seventeen. Time to grow up a little, right?

As I pour a cup of coffee, I wonder if Dad might possibly remember what day it is. Maybe he's calling out a "Happy Birthday" to me from beyond the blue right this minute. Or is everything so incredibly exciting and amazing up there that no one thinks about such mundane things as birthdays anymore? Besides, I think I recall hearing that there are no clocks in heaven. Maybe there are no calendars either.

It feels even colder today than yesterday, and the front lawn is crispy white with frost. I'm about to turn up the thermostat, but instead I decide to build a fire again. A birthday fire. And maybe it's because I was thinking of Dad, but I also decide to make myself a birthday breakfast just like he would've done if he were still here. Not just a bowl of cold cornflakes for this girl. I even get out the big electric griddle that hasn't seen daylight in ages and mix up some instant pancakes and even fry up a couple of eggs to go with it—might as well load up on cholesterol while I'm still young.

I pour myself a glass of orange juice, then carry my birthday breakfast over to my now crackling fire to eat. Okay, it's a little lonely and some might think it's a little pathetic, but it's not like I'm obsessing over the fact that no one seems to care that it's my birthday. In fact, I'm actually sort of enjoying it.

Then after I finish my food, which is really pretty good, I just sit there watching the fire as it flickers and jumps. The dancing motion of the flames is almost hypnotic. And suddenly I feel something changing, sort of like the couch beneath me is shifting, tipping slightly sideways, although it's not. And then like a flash of lightning, I see something—something that's not really there. And I realize it's a vision! I try to calm myself as I focus.

I continue staring toward the fire, but what I see is entirely different than the bright orange flames. I see a foggy scene, somber and gray, with a dark railroad bridge, the kind with ironwork that looks a little like lace, and it stretches across a raging brown river below. I think I recognize the spot, not far from Kentwick Park, a place where people like to go rafting and boating in the summer, when the air is warm and the river is calm. But it's not summer in this scene, and then I notice something else—there, standing in the center of the bridge, perched on the outer edge, is a person. His arms are behind him, holding on to the bridge, but he's leaning forward. Precariously so. And then this person is jumping—and free-falling down almost as if in slow motion.

I can tell it's a guy with dark brown hair, but I can't see his face well enough to know who it is, although I sense real desperation in his expression. His eyes are tightly closed, and his mouth is grim. But something about him is familiar. And yet...I don't get it. And then, just like that, it's over. Gone. No more vision.

I ponder this, trying to discern what it means. I know with certainty that it's from God because I can just tell—I feel it deep inside of me. And while it was a scary scene, I don't feel frightened. But I do feel an urgency, like I need to do something. But I don't know what. I do know that there

must be a specific purpose for the vision because that's
how God works. But other than that, I am blank.

The more I run it through my head, the less it seems
to make sense. Naturally, I think of Peter Clark since he
and his family have been on my mind lately. And I remember his photos and that he did have dark brown hair.
Could that have been him in the vision? And if so, why?
It doesn't really compute. I mean, Peter's death was
caused by a gunshot wound to the head, not by jumping
from a bridge. And even though I got the strong impression that this guy was killing himself, it wasn't how Peter
died. What is that supposed to mean?

I finally decide to call Ebony. I'll give her the details
while they're still fresh in my mind. Or, if necessary, I'll just
leave a message. Maybe she can make sense of it or perhaps even use it for another case. I call her on my cell
phone and am relieved to hear her answer in person.
I quickly relay the vision with all the details, even down to
where I think the location could be.

"And you think it was Peter in the vision?" she asks
for clarification.

"I don't know. That part was unclear. It could've been
him. Or not. But if it was him, it doesn't really make much
sense, does it?"

There's a long pause, and I can imagine her pondering
this with her eyes slightly narrowed, lips pressed together,
deep in thought. "Maybe Peter considered taking his life
by jumping from a bridge. And maybe that's God's way of
showing us that he actually did intend to take his own life."

Somehow her voice doesn't convince me. It's like she's saying what she thinks I want to hear. "Do you really think so?"

"I don't know, Samantha. To be honest, that whole suicide thing doesn't ring true to me anymore. I've been checking out that suicide website and trying to piece this whole thing together, and I just don't know what to think. Something isn't right."

"Then my suicide vision probably doesn't help much, at least in regard to Peter."

"Hey, at least God is communicating with you again," she says in a brighter tone. "You must be happy about that."

"Actually, I am." Then I tell her that it's my birthday and that I think maybe God wanted to use the vision as a present for me, to show me that He's still going to use me. It's exciting. "I'm sure that would sound crazy to some people. I mean, having a vision about someone jumping off a bridge isn't exactly cheerful."

"I know, but it must be encouraging to know that God still trusts you with this sort of thing, Samantha."

"It is."

"And happy birthday!"

"Thanks." I feel a little silly now, like I shouldn't have told her about my birthday. "I'll let you know if anything else comes up, now that I know the door is open again. Or at least I think it is…I hope it is."

"Maybe 'break time' is over."

I sort of laugh. "Cool."

Then we say good-bye, and I pick up my dirty breakfast dishes and clean up the kitchen. I'm still replaying the vision and trying to understand what it all means as I wipe down the countertops. Then I go to my room, thinking I'll do a little online research about suicide.

Okay, it's a grim subject. No doubt about that. But I am curious as to why anyone would want to end it all. I mean, I can get bummed sometimes, but I would never want to take my own life. That seems like a slap in the face to our Creator. And frankly, I just don't get it. But I'm curious about that suicide website and what kind of information is really available there.

Once I've spent some time reading, I feel shocked and slightly depressed. So many heartbreaking feelings and situations—things I never would've believed if I hadn't read them with my own eyes. Very sad.

"Hey, you!" Olivia bursts into my room holding an *enormous* bunch of helium balloons. *"Happy Birthday!"*

I nearly fall off my chair from the shock. "Who let you in?"

She releases the balloons in my room then hugs me. "I knocked and no one answered. Since I know where the key is, I just let myself in."

"Well, you nearly gave me a heart attack," I say, turning off my computer screen. Then I stand, and realizing that at least one person remembered what day it is, I hug her and thank her for the balloons.

"Please tell me you're not doing homework on your birthday."

"Homework would be a piece of cake compared to what I was just doing," I admit.

Of course, this only makes her extremely curious, so I explain about my vision of the bridge and the jumper. This is followed by my general confusion about suicide, and then, still horrified over what I've just read, I unload on her about the gruesome website I've been visiting.

"They have a website like that?" she says. "How is that even legal?"

"It's the Internet. Who knows? Ebony's the one who told me about it, so it's not like the police aren't aware. And remember I told you about Peter leaving his suicide note through a site like this?"

"You'd think his parents could sue someone." Of course, her dad's an attorney so she would naturally go this direction. But maybe she has a point.

"Well, anyway," I continue, "I was just in this chat room where people ask for advice on how to kill themselves and actually get answers, including medical advice describing which poisons or gases or whatever means are most effective, or least painful, or cheap, or less messy, or more daring, or whatever. It's totally appalling. And everyone is so positive about death and dying. It's like they all encourage each other to just be brave and do it—like they'll be some kind of hero afterward."

"And really, they'll just be dead," Olivia says sadly. "Standing before God and trying to explain why they did what they did. Swell."

I nod. "Isn't that weird to think about? I mean, what would it be like if you just checked out and suddenly discovered there was a whole lot more going on than you realized? It's not like you can change your mind."

"Yeah, I'll bet a lot of them will be, like, 'Oops, I had no idea that You were real, God. Maybe I should've thought this through a little better.'"

"And what do you think God will do?"

She shrugs. "I don't know…what do you think?"

I consider this. "Well, I honestly believe that God is a whole lot more gracious than we give Him credit for. And I think some of these people, like Peter Clark for instance, were probably really confused and hurting and depressed. And for all we know he could've been a Christian, too. I mean, who can see into a person's heart besides God?"

I let out a big sigh. "I guess I hope that God will take all these things into consideration, and I'm sure that heaven will hold some great surprises."

Olivia nods. "Yeah, I'd like to believe that too. Still, I don't get why some people think it's okay to run a website like that. I mean, really, what's their point? Are they just wicked? Or really mean? Or just plain ignorant?"

"There was even a long paragraph about how suicide is a way to support zero population growth."

"Give me a break!"

"No, it's true. And there were links to some zero population websites as well. And one of the girls writing actually sounded pretty sincere. She seemed convinced that the world is too populated and like she'd be doing everyone a favor by checking out."

"No way! She really believes she can help control the world's population by killing herself?" asks Olivia incredulously. "I so don't get that."

"I know. It makes you wonder if murder won't be next on the list. I mean, if these guys are really worried about the globe getting crowded but they happen to be having a good day or a good life, would they consider taking out their neighbor just to keep the numbers down?"

"Especially if that neighbor's on the obnoxious side, plays his rap music a little too loud, or has a dog that poops on your freshly mowed lawn."

"But really," I say, "it's not something we should joke about. I mean, these people sound dead serious—and I'm not saying that to be funny. It was really depressing. Like there was this one foster kid who was so depressed that he wanted to kill himself, but he was concerned about another foster kid, a four-year-old girl, who lived in the same home. He thought she might freak if she discovered him dead, that she might be messed up for life. But someone told him not to worry about it, just get the deed done and let that poor little girl fend for herself. One girl named Slinky actually told him he was providing a good role model and that when that little girl grew up and decided to kill herself, she'd have him to thank. Can you believe it?"

"That is seriously sick."

"Tell me about it."

"And *that* is what you're doing on your birthday, Sam?"

"Pretty pathetic, huh?"

Now Olivia gets a thoughtful look. "So can *anyone* respond to those messages? Or do you have to be a registered member of the death club and pay your dues or sign something in blood or maybe join the Hemlock Society first?"

So I flick my monitor back on, returning to the disgusting suicide website, and we find out that they're open to new members. In fact, they encourage it. So Olivia and I both register, under different names, of course. Olivia is Hope, and I am Grace. Okay, maybe that sounds a bit trite, but this is serious business—these people *need* some hope and grace.

Then we sit together at my desk and start creating what we think might be encouraging messages. Of course, there's no way to know how they will be received since some of these morbid death wishers have a real attitude going on. But we figure it's worth our best shot, and some of our words feel downright inspired, at least to us. By the time we're done, we both feel much better about ourselves and the people we've attempted to communicate some sense to. Then we actually pray, by name, for the people we just wrote to.

"Thanks," I tell her. "That was pretty cool."

"We'll have to check back later and see if anyone was tuning in."

"Do you think some people are just trying to unload?" I say. "Maybe just a cry for attention and they're not really serious about suicide?"

"I suppose anything's possible, but if I wanted attention, I think I'd find a different kind of website. One that might care about me personally and offer answers that could really help. That one seems to celebrate suicide like it's heroic, like it's going to be the end-all of everyone's problems." She grabs me by the hand. "Now we need to get out of this funk. This is *your* birthday, Sam. We need to go have some fun."

"Suggestions?"

"Well, I wanted to get you something, but I was torn. And then I thought, *What would I want someone to do for me*?"

"And?"

"And I thought, *Let's go shopping.* I want you to pick out your birthday present. Okay?"

I grin. "Sounds good. I think I'd like a red Ferrari."

"Yeah, right. Okay, put on some real clothes and let's get out of this gloomy room."

"Hey, it's not a gloomy room." I point to the cheerful balloons splayed across my ceiling like a three-dimensional mosaic.

"Okay, it's not your room, but you have to admit that website was gloomy. In fact, I think we might need to do a cleansing prayer for your room, Sam. You know, to get rid of any yucky spirits that might try to hang around and creep you out in the middle of the night."

I consider this and think she might have a point, but before I can even respond, Olivia has closed her eyes and, with hands held up, is praying over my room. I suppress a snicker as she gets fairly dramatic, telling the foul spirits to split in the name of Jesus.

"Amen!" she says.

"Amen!" I echo, actually laughing now. "Sorry. I know this is serious business, but you're pretty funny too."

"Yeah, yeah. Come on, Sam." She grabs me by the hands and pulls me to my feet. "Let's get moving. Time's a wasting."

So I get it together, and Olivia drives us to the local mall. And as usual, shopping with this girl is great. Seriously, I don't think anyone could have a bad time shopping with her. Not only does she have a sense of humor along with some really good fashion instincts and, oh yeah, deep pockets, but she's also really encouraging about my own personal image issues.

For instance, if I think my rear end looks like a double-wide in a certain pair of jeans, she'll first assure me that I'm totally wrong about the dimensions of my derrière, but then she'll help me to find a better pair of jeans that end up looking totally awesome. That is a true friend.

Seven

For my birthday present, we finally zoom in on shoes. According to Olivia, a girl can never have too many shoes. And after trying on everything from patent leather stilettos to some real earth muffin sandals, I finally settle on the coolest boots imaginable. Of course, they cost too much, but as the frazzled saleswoman points out, *they are on sale*.

"You *have* to get them," Olivia says as I parade around in them. "You look totally awesome in them."

"Even on sale, they're too much," I protest as I admire them in the short mirror. But Olivia refuses to take no for an answer. Finally the deal is done, the boots are bagged, and we go get some lunch. Olivia insists on treating.

"Thanks for everything," I tell her as we head for home. "You're way too nice to me."

"Only on your birthday," she teases. "I can be a real beast for the rest of the year."

"Yeah, right!" I laugh. Seriously, I can't imagine having a better best friend than Olivia.

"I'll pick you up at six-thirty," she says as she drops me at my house.

"Huh?"

"For your birthday surprise."

"I thought *this* was my birthday surprise."

"There's more." She winks. "And wear something nice, okay? Like those new boots and your Banana Republic corduroy skirt. That'll look good."

"Okay," I say with uncertainty. Then she zips off, and as I'm walking to the house still wondering about what lies ahead for this evening, I notice a bouquet of flowers by the front door.

Okay, this day just keeps getting better and better! I'm sort of hoping the pretty blooms are from Conrad, but they end up being from Ebony and some others down at city hall, which is actually quite nice.

I go inside and put my things away, and just as I'm going back downstairs, I suddenly experience another flash. It feels similar to the one by the fire this morning. But it comes so quickly that I actually stop midstep, pausing right there on the stairs to see whether it's for real or not. It is.

This vision is brief—maybe just a couple seconds or less—but it appears to involve the same guy—at least the dark brown hair looks the same. Only this time he's in a room, just a nondescript room, but I can tell it's inside a building or a house. And he's wearing what appears to be a gas mask, although I'm not totally sure that's what it is. It reminds me of something from an old war movie, and it actually looks kind of scary. Surrounding the edges of this mask is what looks like silver duct tape, as if the guy is try-ing to seal the mask even tighter to his face. Then I notice a tube protruding from the side of the gas mask, being held in place by more duct tape. This tube connects to a bright orange metal canister. That's it. And the vision leaves as quickly as it came, about as fast as the snap of my fingers.

Still, once it's gone, I feel slightly stunned and grab the handrail to steady myself. Then I actually sit on the stairs to think about what I just saw, to figure out what it might mean. But once again, it makes no sense. And once again, I'm assuming that this guy is Peter, although this also makes no sense.

At first I think he's using the gas mask to protect himself from the air around him. Maybe that orange tank contained oxygen. But then I remember from chemistry class that oxygen tanks are usually green. For some reason it seems important to figure out what was in that tank, so I head for my computer and Google selections of words like "orange gas tanks," but only find weird things like "put an orange in your gas tank to improve your gas mileage." Yeah, right.

Finally, I give up and just lean back in my chair and let out a long sigh. I notice the colorful balloons happily floating above my head and suddenly remember the times I've helped my mom during the Summer Festival for the park district. Zach and I usually competed over the fun job of filling the balloons with helium—and the big tank we used to fill them was orange.

Was the guy in my vision trying to breathe helium? And if so, why? Did he want to float away? Or was he trying to kill himself?

I return to my computer and Google "helium poisoning" and discover that there have been a couple of suicides done this way recently. I also learn that the website Olivia and I visited earlier today contains the instructions for how to commit suicide this way. But what does this mean?

It's already after five o'clock, and I have no idea whether Ebony is still at city hall, but I decide to give her a call anyway. I get her voice mail and leave a detailed message about my latest vision and what I discovered about helium poisoning online. "Of course, I don't know what this means," I admit, "what the significance is… But I thought I should tell you about it." After I hang up, I decide it's time to write down the two visions I've had today. So I put them in my notebook, much in the way I did when I was helping Ebony with Kayla's case. Maybe it has nothing to do with anything, which I doubt, but just in case, I want to be ready.

Then I decide to go back to the suicide website to see if anyone has read or responded to the messages written by "Grace" and "Hope" today. And man oh man, are there responses! And to say that they are not very nice responses is a *huge* understatement. It seems we've hit a real sore spot with a bunch of mixed-up death-wishing people. As much as we attempted to come across as loving, kind, and gracious, we have been pathetically misunderstood by most of the members of that website.

My hands actually begin to shake as I read some of the posts. Olivia and I are regarded as "intruders" who "have no *blanking* right to interfere" with their website. We're told to "drop dead" or "get a life" or "butt out." Of course, a lot of four-letter words are interspersed in these angry posts, as well as lots more derogatory and hateful remarks. One less hostile girl simply calls us "misguided, ignorant evangelists who should mind your *blanking* business." But a guy named Mort says, "It's *blanked*-up *blanks* like Grace and Hope who *blank* up the world, making normal people like me and my friends want to take a flying leap from the *blanked*-up planet."

Finally, I can't take any more, and I exit the site without making any new comments. Maybe it was a mistake to try to get involved in something like this. I'm just glad that we used fake names and no one knows how to track us down. I can't imagine what it would be like to meet one of these people face-to-face.

This reminds me of Peter, and I can't imagine how a guy like him—who looked so normal in his photos—could've been comfortable spending time at a site like that. But then I know that people are full of surprises and sometimes what we see on the surface is simply that—the surface. Still, it makes me so sad for Peter. Sad that he got sucked into a site like that, sad that he bought in to their lies and hopelessness, sad that he actually fell for it by taking his own life. If he did take his life...and despite what Ebony is thinking, I am feeling more certain that this is probably the case. Maybe these visions, while they never really happened, might be things Peter considered before he took his dad's gun and shot himself.

But this disturbs me. In fact, it disturbs me a lot. And I'm not sure I really want to face the reason it disturbs me. I especially don't want to face it on my birthday. Consequently I try to distract myself by taking a nice long shower and getting ready for whatever it is Olivia has in mind for tonight. She's right about the Banana Republic skirt. It is perfect with the boots. I top off my outfit with a white T-shirt and a brown lacy cardigan sweater, then check it out in the mirror. Not bad!

"Samantha!" says my mom, knocking on my door in an urgent way. I didn't even know she was home.

"What?" I jerk open the door, preparing myself for the worst. Maybe it's Zach. Has he done—?

"Oh, sweetheart!" She explodes into my room, throwing her arms around me. "I totally forgot your birthday!"

"Is that all?" I step back and study her, certain that there must be something more. Something really serious must be wrong.

"Yes, I just got home and saw the flowers from Ebony, and it hit me like a ton of bricks. I totally forgot!" She actually has tears in her eyes now. "I am the worst mother on earth, Sam. How could I possibly forget my own daughter's birth—?"

"It's okay, Mom. I understand. You've been busy. Life's hard. It's okay, really."

Mom sniffs then nods. "Well, it's *not* okay. But I'm glad you understand." Then she actually seems to see me. "Oh, by the way, you look nice. Big date tonight?"

"I'm not sure. Olivia is up to something."

"Are those new boots?"

I glance down at my extra-cool footwear and nod.

She frowns. "Where'd you get them?"

"Olivia got them for me, for my birthday."

"Oh…" I can tell by Mom's expression that she's not so sure about this. "They look expensive."

"They were on sale."

"Oh…"

"Olivia wouldn't let me leave Nordstrom without them."

"I guess Olivia can afford to be extravagant."

Okay, this comment irks me a little or maybe it's just the tone she's using, but it sounds like a put-down. Still, I refuse to let it get to me. "Olivia is a good friend and a generous person."

"Well, I am sorry I forgot your birthday, Sam." She presses her lips together. "How about if I make it up to you next weekend when we go shopping? We'll really make a day of it."

"Sounds great." I glance at my watch. "Uh, Olivia should be here any minute."

"Then I won't keep you." Mom backs out of my room. "Have a good time."

As it turns out, I do have a good time. In fact, I have a fantastic time. Much to my surprise, Olivia made reservations at a new French restaurant in town. I naturally assume it's just her and me. And that's cool. But as we walk across the extremely sophisticated restaurant, I notice some familiar faces sitting at a table for four right next to the gas-burning fireplace. Olivia has prearranged to have our dates, Conrad and Alex, already there waiting for us.

"Happy birthday," Conrad says as he stands to greet and hug me, popping a little kiss on my cheek. Then he presents me with a clear plastic box containing a wrist corsage of pale pink tea roses. A little corny, but very sweet.

"Thank you!" I say as he helps me remove my coat and I slip on the flowers.

"Happy birthday." Alex hands me a card.

"This is so cool." I sit down and feel like queen of the party.

"Are you really surprised?" asks Olivia.

"Of course! This is incredible, Olivia!"

Then since the owner of the restaurant is a friend of Olivia's dad, we are all treated like celebrities. They even bring us a complimentary bottle of sparkling cider, complete with a silver ice bucket. The waiter serves this in tall champagne flutes—very classy. And I feel so grown-up. I can tell this is going to be a night I will always remember. And even though I still have a few sad but fleeting thoughts about Peter, the suicide site, and the gloomy visions I've had today, this little dinner party proves to be a good distraction from those somber things. The four of us laugh and joke and practice our French.

"I want to go to France someday," I tell them.

"Me too," says Olivia. "We should plan a trip to Europe after graduation."

"That'd be awesome," I say. "Maybe I better start saving now."

"Are boys allowed?" teases Conrad.

"Hmm, I don't know…" I study Conrad as if I'm seriously weighing this.

"Graduation is a long way off," Olivia says lightly. "That gives us plenty of time to think about whether our European trip is open to guys or not."

After we finish dinner, which includes espresso and an incredible dark chocolate dessert with a name I still can't pronounce, and after Olivia takes care of the bill (which her dad is actually paying for), we decide to split up and go our separate ways.

Olivia's plan seemed to be to have Conrad drive me home in his funky Gremlin, which is fine with me. Meanwhile Alex was supposed to hitch a ride with Olivia in her much cooler and newer Toyota Camry. But I'm actually glad to be with Conrad. And I know Olivia is happy to be with Alex. I just hope Alex is okay with it. It's hard to read that boy sometimes, and I occasionally worry that he's just getting roped into our little foursome for the sake of convenience. I worry that he might end up telling Olivia that he's not interested in her, and she is just too nice of a girl to be hurt by something like that. Still, I'm not sure there's much I can do about it.

"Did you have a good time tonight?" Conrad asks as he drives through town.

I turn and smile at him. "I had a great time. Thanks for coming and everything."

"I still have something for you." He stops at a red light.

"Huh?"

"A birthday present."

"But you already gave me my roses..."

"That was just for fun, Samantha. Besides, those flowers won't last long."

I'm not so sure about that since I've already decided to dry them and save them as a memento from this perfect evening. I sigh happily, leaning back into the sheepskin-covered seat. Conrad is driving across the overpass now, the one that goes above the freeway. But up ahead, midway across the overpass, I see someone standing on the edge of the cement safety barrier. He's illuminated by the head-lights, and his hands are held out, as if he's going to jump.

"Oh my gosh!" I suddenly sit forward and point at the dark-haired young man who's about to jump.

"What?" Conrad starts to brake the car. "Is something in the road?"

"Don't you see him?" I cry out. Then as quickly as the image appeared, it now vanishes, and I suddenly realize it wasn't real. Just a vision. I should've known. Why didn't I keep my mouth shut?

Conrad is going very slowly now. "See *what*?"

"Oh, it's gone now," I say quickly. "Sorry about that."

"But what was it?"

I obviously need to explain myself, but I can't tell him the truth, that I have visions and dreams, or that God speaks to me in some pretty unusual ways. "I just thought I saw something," I say quietly. "Sorry."

"You said *him*. Did you see a person?"

"I think it was an animal." I feel guilty for the lie. "Something going across the road. I just called it *him*, well, just because I did. But now that I think about it, I bet it was just a shadow or something."

He shakes his head. "Man, I didn't see a thing."

"Or who knows? Maybe I imagined the whole thing. Let's just be glad it was nothing, okay?"

He nods. "That works for me. You know, my dad's always warning me to be careful with the Gremlin since it'd be really hard to find replacement parts if I ever get into a wreck."

"You'd think he'd be more concerned about your welfare if you got in a wreck."

He laughs. "Yeah, well, I guess that's implied."

Once we're at my house, Conrad opens his glove compartment and retrieves a small, neatly wrapped box. And suddenly I feel nervous. I mean, I'm not the kind of girl who's used to dating, not to mention getting gifts from guys—especially gifts in boxes that look as if they might contain jewelry.

"I wasn't sure what to get you—"

"You didn't need to get me any—"

"I wanted to, Samantha."

I nod and smile. "Okay."

"I wasn't sure you'd like it, but I asked Olivia and she gave me the thumbs-up."

"Olivia knows me pretty well."

He hands me the box. "Go ahead and open it."

I carefully remove the paper, and it does turn out to be a velvet-covered jewelry box. I am getting really nervous again. What if it's something really expensive? What should I do? Give it back and risk hurting his feelings? But to keep an expensive gift, especially if it was, like, something with diamonds... Well, that would seem all wrong. I glance nervously at him.

"Aren't you going to open it?"

I force a laugh. "Sorry...I guess I was just trying to pro-long my birthday." Then I open the box and am pleased to see that no diamonds are involved. It's a short silver chain with something hanging from it. I hold it up to the dome light to see it better.

"It's a charm bracelet. But I could only afford one charm. It's supposed to represent your birthday." He points to the small silver charm with something red in the center. "The saleslady said that's your birthstone."

"A garnet?"

"Yeah, that's right. And I had them engrave the year on the back. That way you can always remember this night." He looks earnestly at me. "Do you like it?"

I grin and throw my arms around him. "I love it!"

Then he kisses me and sighs. "Oh, good. I was wor-ried that you might think it was goofy. I mean, first that cor-sage and then a charm bracelet? You might think I have some kind of wrist fetish."

I laugh. "I do not think it's goofy, and I'm sure you don't have a wrist fetish. And Olivia was right—a charm bracelet is perfect. I can't wait to start filling it up."

"Yeah, the saleslady showed me all kinds of charms. They have something for every imaginable occasion—and even for some you can't imagine."

"Cool." Then I hold the bracelet out to him. "Want to help me put it on?"

So he fumbles with it and finally it's on and I hold it up in the light. "What do you think?"

He grins. "I think it looks great on you."

So I thank him again and he walks me to the door, kisses me good night, and I go inside the house. This has been the best day ever.

Okay, I'm thinking as I head for my room it's also been a little heavy due to the whole suicide thing. And then I consider that last vision and the guy on the overpass and, well, I'm not quite sure what I'm supposed to think. For whatever reason—and this has me seriously concerned—God seems to want me tuned in to suicide. Maybe it has to do with Peter...or maybe something else. But I'll record it in my notebook, and I will make an appointment to see Ebony on Monday.

Eight

So what do we have here?" Ebony asks me on Monday after school. "Three visions of what appear to be methods of suicide?"

"Yes." I glance down at my notes. "One jumping from a bridge. One asphyxiating himself by what I think is helium, and one jumping from the overpass."

"And you said you read that helium has been used for suicide?"

"It didn't sound common, but at least a couple of deaths. And that site gave explicit instructions on how to do it."

"And that was how it appeared in your vision?"

"It seemed to be the case."

Ebony peers at me with intense brown eyes. "And what do you think of all this, Samantha?"

I frown. "To be honest, I'm getting a little spooked."

Her brows arch. "Spooked?"

"Yeah…" I glance away, unsure that I really want to go there. Although if I can't be up front with Ebony, who's left? I know for a fact that my mom doesn't want to hear about this. Even though she's aware that I'm working with Ebony on "something new," she's made it clear that it's up to me and Ebony to keep things "under control" and that she really doesn't want to hear about it—period. And although Olivia has been very supportive, this might be more than she can handle right now. Especially considering the fact that Alex just gave her the official "we're not a couple" speech yesterday after church. She's been seriously bummed all day.

"What's up, Samantha? What's making you feel spooked?"

I take a deep breath and slowly exhale. "Well, you know how I always have to make it clear to anyone involved in any of these cases that I am *not* a medium or psychic?"

She nods. "You always do a good job of setting people straight."

I hold up my hands. "So what's up with this?"

"What?" She looks confused.

"Why am I having visions of dead people?"

She frowns. "Is that what you think they are?"

"Well, I sort of assumed the guy in my visions is Peter. I mean, I can never see his face clearly. But his hair is right. The build seems right. And he's the only guy I know who supposedly killed himself. It all seems to fit."

"Okay, let's say these visions are of Peter. Why do you think you're having them? What is God trying to show us?"

I know she won't want to hear my answer, but all I can say is the truth—or what I believe is the truth. And I know what I am beginning to believe. It seems to make sense. "Basically, I think the visions are God's way of showing us that Peter really did kill himself."

She folds her arms across her front and leans back in her chair without saying a word. Her expression is hard to read. It might be that she's skeptical, or perhaps she's simply disappointed.

But whether or not she wants to hear this, I have to get my story out—the sooner the better. "I think Peter spent a lot of time on that suicide website. He might've been one of those guys asking lots of questions and trying to get advice. And during that time, I think he probably considered all the various ways he could kill himself. And maybe he even attempted a few of them."

"Such as what you saw in your visions?"

"Exactly." I start speaking faster now, almost as if it's all starting to jell for me even as I'm telling it. "So maybe Peter really did go up on that bridge by Kentwick Park, and maybe he did consider jumping, but something caused him to stop. Maybe he saw someone. Or maybe he suddenly realized he was afraid of heights or that the water would be freezing cold."

"If he really wanted to die, would he even care?"

"Who knows? But it seems possible. It also seems possible that Peter could have gone out and purchased an army surplus gas mask and some duct tape and rented a tank of helium and tried to do himself in like that. Although according to what I've read online, that's a really uncomfortable way to die."

She just shakes her head and rolls her eyes. "This is all so pitiful."

"I know, I know, but stick with me here. And remember that you're the one who asked what I thought. So maybe Peter decided to nix the helium poisoning idea, but he still wanted to kill himself. What if he went onto the overpass, the same one in my vision, and it was nighttime? Maybe he stood there and considered leaping, but perhaps he looked down and saw the nonstop flow of the traffic, all those lights streaming along at sixty-plus miles an hour. What if he didn't want anyone driving below to get hurt by his body smashing through their windshield at that kind of speed? I mean, that's pretty gruesome if you think about it. Consequently he changed his mind again."

"You really think Peter could've done all that?"

"I don't know, Ebony. I'm just trying to work with what I've got. And so maybe Peter got tired of all his failed attempts at suicide. It's possible that there were even more than what I've seen in my visions. And maybe one day, like if he was just having this really bad day, he suddenly remembered his dad's gun in the drawer by the bed, and suddenly it all seemed perfectly clear. So simple and quick."

"And so he shot himself in the head. The end," finishes Ebony in an exasperated voice.

"I know that's not going to help with the case you're trying to develop."

"I'm not trying to *develop* anything."

"Okay. But I realize my visions do not support the possible murder theory."

"No, you're right. They don't."

"I'm sorry…"

She almost smiles. "Don't be sorry, Samantha. I'm not mad at you. Remember, you're just the messenger here. You can't help what messages are being sent."

"I know…" I look back down at my notes, trying to see if there might be something I missed hidden in there somewhere. But it looks just the same as before. And it seems pretty plain to me.

Part of me feels better for having gotten it out. But I do *not* feel good. In fact, a real sense of heaviness is settling onto me, almost as if a load of bricks is being strapped across my shoulders. I'm not sure if it's because my visions seem to be of no use to Ebony, or because I'm still feeling confused about this whole thing in general. Whatever it is, it's overwhelming. And it suddenly seems ironic that less than a week ago, I was longing for God to give me a vision or a dream—of any sort. I was begging for Him to communicate with me. And now that I've had several visions…well, I seem to be buckling under the weight. Maybe I'm really not cut out for this. Maybe God was trying to show me that.

Ebony clears her throat. "As far as the medium/psychic thing goes…"

I look up. "Yeah?"

"Do you want to know what I think?"

"Of course!"

"Well, I believe that Scripture is clear that we are not supposed to communicate with the dead."

"That's just what worries me."

"But you don't know for a fact that was the case, Samantha."

"But it seemed like it was Peter. And you have to admit, my hypothesis makes sense. Peter was on that website. He might've followed some of that crazy advice and made several failed attempts on his life."

"Yes, he might have."

"But you don't think so?"

"I don't know. What I do know is that I believe God has given you a gift, Samantha. Do you believe that yourself?"

I nod. "Yes."

"And I don't believe that God would give you a gift that contradicts what He has told us in Scripture. Do you?"

I shake my head. "It doesn't sound like God to me."

"And we know that Peter is dead. So we probably need to assume, based on Scripture, that God would not allow you to receive messages from him, *right*?"

"Right."

"So perhaps you're jumping to a conclusion, thinking you've been seeing Peter in your visions. Maybe it's not."

I consider this. "Just a coincidence then?"

"It might be simply because I've told you about Peter and you've been in his home and you're concerned for his mom and brother. It's not terribly surprising that you would assume those visions were about him."

"But the hair color was—"

"How many people have dark brown hair?" She points to my head. "Even you do."

"But mine's curly. The guy in my vision had straight hair."

She smiles. "Okay, how many people have dark brown hair that's straight?"

"Probably a lot." I smile.

"Anyway, my conclusion is that the guy in your visions was *not* Peter."

I think about this. "So, if it wasn't Peter, and we've established that I'm *not* a medium and I'm *not* getting messages from the dead—*thank goodness!*—then it seems like we'd have to assume that the guy in my visions is still alive, right?"

"Bingo."

"But how long will he continue to be alive?"

"Good question."

"I wonder if the guy is participating in that website…" Then I tell Ebony about the messages Olivia and I posted under our pseudonyms. I also tell her about the horrible responses we received. "Do you think God is warning me about one of them?"

"It's possible." She's reaching for a file now, and I'm worried that I have taken up way too much of her time.

"I'm sorry to go on and on," I say, standing.

"It's okay, Samantha."

"But it hasn't helped you at all."

"Perhaps not on Peter's case. But if it helps with someone else who's planning to kill himself, well, I can't complain about that."

"I wish I could help you with Peter's case."

"Like you said, you're not a medium." Ebony winks.

"But God's big. He works in lots of different ways. I'll try to stay open, okay?"

She smiles. "Okay." Then as I'm going out the door she adds, "And if you do figure out who that other suicidal guy is, be sure and give me a call. I'll do what I can to help. Even if it's across the state line we can still get in touch with the authorities there."

I thank her and leave. And okay, I feel a little bit better now. It seems to lighten the load to realize that the guy in my visions was *not* Peter. At least, I think I agree with Ebony on this. But now I have to ask myself—who was that guy? Is he still alive? And what can I do to help him if I don't even know him? It's pretty mind-boggling.

As I walk down Main Street toward the Lava Java coffee shop, I observe a guy with straight dark brown hair walking directly toward me. *Could that be him?* He appears to be in his twenties and nicely dressed. Then he notices me staring at him and smiles. Good grief, he probably thinks I'm flirting with him. So I glance away. Great. Now I'll be obsessing over every guy I meet with hair like that. And I'm sure Ebony's right; there are probably a lot of them.

I pause in front of Lava Java and dial Olivia's cell phone number. She dropped me off in town after school, and despite her aching heart, she generously offered to pick me up afterward. After a couple of rings, I hear her voice, but it doesn't sound like her normal happy self. I can tell she's still feeling bummed about Alex.

"Hey, Olivia," I say extra cheerfully. "Can I buy you a cup of joe?"

"You need a ride?"

"If it's not too much trouble."

"No, I'm on my way."

"Thanks." I hang up and sigh. Poor Olivia. Good thing she doesn't have straight dark brown hair, or I might get really worried. Of course, I suppose she'd have to be a guy too. I go inside and order two mochas with extra whipped cream. This is a day for indulgences.

When Olivia comes into Lava Java, her expression is the same as it's been all day. Totally bummed. And it actually looks like her heels are dragging too. Really, it's breaking my heart.

"Livvie," I say when she sits down. "You look so sad."

She fakes a smile. "That better?"

I push the mocha toward her. "Maybe some caffeine will improve your spirits."

She takes a sip. "So how did it go with Ebony?"

I decide to go ahead and fill her in. If nothing else it might help to distract her from her Alex blues. And she'll probably appreciate my relief and that I'm not stressed over the whole medium thing now.

"So if it's not Peter, who is it?" she asks after I finish. And I think I detect the tiniest bit of genuine interest.

"That's the big question. Because I'm sure it's someone. God wouldn't send me such clear messages just to jerk me around. So now I'm on the lookout for any guy with dark brown straight hair. I almost accosted a perfect stranger on the street—"

"Alex has dark brown hair," she says suddenly. "And it's straight too."

"But Alex isn't depressed—"

"Maybe he is," she says a little too eagerly. "I mean, you can't always tell by the way people act. And if you ask me, he's acting a little strange. Maybe there are things going on inside him that we don't know about; maybe he's hiding his feelings."

"About what?"

Her brow creases as she gives this her full attention. "Well, he's mentioned being concerned about his parents' marriage problems."

"But seriously, would he or anyone else commit suicide over that?"

"Maybe not."

"I really don't think he's depressed, Olivia."

"Maybe not." She sighs. "Guess I'm the one who's depressed."

"I know it's hard. But you *will* get over this."

She looks up at me with sad blue eyes. "Why doesn't he like me, Sam?"

I shrug. "I have absolutely no idea. I think any guy in his right mind would love you. Even Conrad can't figure it out."

"I wish I could just hate him and be done with it. Okay, maybe not *hate* him, that's pretty strong, but I really wish I could dislike him a lot. Why is it that being dumped doesn't just automatically make you despise that person?"

"I don't know..."

"I mean, he didn't exactly *dump* me, because we weren't really dating, well, other than with you and Conrad. And to be fair, he was rather sweet about it. He said he just didn't want to be serious with *anyone* right now." She gets that extremely worried expression again. "Do you think it's because he actually *is* the guy in your vision? What if he's really depressed and trying to sever his relationships because he's planning a suicide?"

"No, I honestly don't think that's what's going on."

"But what if you're wrong, Sam? Remember some of the things we read on that suicide website? People are supposed to cut ties with their loved ones before they check out. How can you be certain that Alex *isn't* the guy in your vision?"

For her sake, I give this my full consideration, but I just can't buy into it. I know that Olivia needs an explanation to make her feel better, but thinking of Alex as suicidal seems totally ridiculous. Still, she looks slightly hopeful, which strikes me as pretty weird. I mean, does she want him to kill himself? No, of course not. She just wants a reason for her heartache.

"I have an idea," I tell her. "How about if I ask Conrad about Alex, without mentioning our suicide concerns. I'll ask Conrad for his take on the whole thing and what he really thinks about Alex and his motives for breaking up with you."

"It wasn't actually a breakup," she says again. I wonder if that makes her feel better.

"Fine, I won't ask about the breakup, okay? I'll ask Conrad about Alex's state of mind and if he, like me, thinks his buddy needs to get his head examined for not wanting to go out with you. Will that work?"

She rolls her eyes then actually smiles. "Well, something to that effect might be acceptable."

Nine

*H*e *just wasn't that into her,"* Conrad tells me for about the third time. I think I've questioned him a little beyond his patience, and I'm surprised he hasn't hung up on me by now.

"Sorry to be such a pest," I say. "But Olivia is taking this so hard... I promised her I'd try to figure it out."

"Well, tell Olivia that it's not because of Alex's parents and it's not because of another girl and it's not because Olivia isn't cool. She is. It's just Alex, okay? He can be like that. He gets his mind set on or against something, and there's no turning that boy back. I guess it can be a good thing, like when it comes to serving God or sports or things that require determination. But I'm pretty sure that he's just not into Olivia."

"Do you think it has anything to do with the fact that she sort of went after him?"

"Maybe..."

"Aha."

"Most guys don't like to be pursued like that. I mean, I suppose it's kinda flattering when a girl likes you so much that she'll go after you, but most guys want to be the ones doing the chasing. I think it has to do with the hunter instinct."

I laugh. "Sort of like the cavemen, out hunting down their women, knocking them over the head with a club then dragging them back to the campfire to whip up some Brontosaurus soup?"

He chuckles. "Yeah, something like that."

This makes me remember how I showed very little interest in Conrad last fall. And it wasn't that I was trying to play hard to get; I was just so focused on finding Kayla that I probably seemed indifferent. Maybe that's what Olivia needs to do—focus on something else.

Conrad and I talk a little more; then I tell him it's getting late and I have homework and better get to it.

"Still playing hard to get, huh?" he teases.

"Seriously, I still have geometry and history."

So we hang up and I hit the books. And some kids might think it's nerdish to cut off a conversation with my boyfriend just to do homework, but the fact is I do take academics pretty seriously. Oh, I'm certainly not like my dedicated lab partner, Garrett Pierson, who's been obsessing over every tiny detail in this week's chemistry project. But I am definitely college-bound, and I do try to keep my grades up. So much so that I've even considered dropping my chemistry class for now. I so don't get it, and it feels like my grade is totally riding on Garrett.

To make matters worse, Garrett, while completely competent, is not very adept at conveying information to me. He tends to take over the projects, only giving me bits and pieces of facts, so that for the most part I'm in the dark. I think I'll try to discuss this with him tomorrow.

After picking me up the next morning, Olivia wants me to tell her everything Conrad told me last night.

"All the details," she insists as she drives toward school. "Don't spare my feelings."

"He really didn't say that much. But it was enough to reassure me that Alex is not suicidal, okay?"

"That's it?" She sounds disappointed.

"Pretty much."

"Don't Alex and Conrad talk? You know, the way we do?"

"I don't know…"

Olivia pounds the steering wheel with her hands. "So that's *it?*"

"Yeah. That, and Conrad said Alex just wasn't that into you."

"Duh."

"But Conrad did have a theory about that."

"About what?" She glances at me.

"Why Alex wasn't that into you."

"What is it?" She sounds way too eager now. "Is there something I can do?"

"See, that's just the problem."

"Huh?"

"You're too eager, Olivia. And Alex probably got scared off."

She lets out a groan.

"Conrad told me that most guys don't like to be chased. They want to be the pursuer."

She nods. "Yeah, you tried to tell me that."

"But you didn't listen."

"I just like him so much, Sam."

"I know."

For the rest of the way to school, we don't say anything. I know she's feeling bad, and I wish there was something I could do to help her, but maybe she just needs to walk through this.

"I'll be praying for you, Olivia," I say as we prepare to part ways at school. "I think God wants to bring something good out of this."

She nods sadly. "Yeah, I hope so."

As I walk to class, I wonder how hearts can get so entangled that people get hurt like that. And I wish Olivia could've been spared. But at the same time, I think she has something to learn here too. And it's not just about how to play hard to get.

She still seems pretty bummed at lunch. So to distract her, I start talking to her about chemistry, my next class, and how I plan to confront Garrett. "And maybe I'll just drop it and take physics next year."

"Yuck." She makes a face. "You want to be stuck with a science class in your senior year?"

I roll my eyes. "I wish I'd followed your example and taken them all before now."

She actually smiles. "Yeah, something I learned from my dad. If it's going to be unpleasant, it's better to just get it over with."

I consider this. "Maybe I'll stick it out in chemistry then."

Even so, I do confront Garrett. And, of course, I hurt his feelings in the process. Or so it seems. Because as soon as I say my little spiel, he instantly clams up and totally ignores me. I just sit there across from him, watching as he furiously pounds today's notes into his laptop—the mad scientist hard at work. Then I notice something. He has straight, dark brown hair. And the way his bangs fall across his forehead and almost into his eyes looks similar to the guy in my vision.

"Garrett," I say suddenly and he looks up.

He doesn't say anything, just stares at me with that wounded expression.

"I'm sorry if I offended you. You are a great lab partner and I really appreciate you, okay? I'm just worried that I'm riding on your coattails here."

He almost smiles. "*My* coattails?"

"You know what I mean. I feel like you're carrying the whole load."

"But that's okay." He looks down at his computer. "I'm used to it."

"What do you mean?"

He shrugs and looks back down, muttering, "Nothing."

"All I'm asking is that you include me, *okay?*"

He looks back up again. "I'll try."

"Thanks." I'm trying not to stare at him now, trying not to obsess over the fact that he might possibly be the guy in my visions.

Ironically, Garrett actually makes a noble attempt at including me in our experiment, but I'm so focused on him and whether or not he's suicidal that I'm totally useless. Consequently, everything he explains goes straight over my head.

Even so, I try to keep the conversation going with him after class ends, walking with him down the hall, although he's going in the opposite direction of my next class. As I'm walking (or is it stalking?), I attempt to ask chemistry-related questions that sound lame even to me. Finally he stops walking and turns and looks at me.

"No offense, Samantha, but you really don't get it, do you?"

"Huh? What?"

"Science."

"Oh." I sort of smile. "Is it that obvious?"

He nods. "So, what's your point here?"

"My point?" Does he know that this isn't about science? Can he sense that I've got a whole different agenda here? I give him my best innocent look.

"Yeah, first you tell me you don't want me to help you in class; then you show how totally ignorant you are... I mean, what am I supposed to do?"

I hold up my hands like I'm surrendering. "Maybe this should be your call. Maybe you'd like a different lab partner. In that case, I think I'll just drop chemistry anyway."

His brows draw together as he considers this. "Well..." He sighs. "I suppose if it really was my choice, which I doubt it is, I'd tell you to stick it out."

"Even if I drag you down?"

He shrugs. "I can handle it."

"Okay then. I'll stick it out."

"Okay then."

"Thanks, Garrett."

He still looks a little stunned, and his face is turning slightly red. I have a strong suspicion that this is the longest conversation he's ever had with a girl.

"See ya," I call as I turn and walk the other way.

Maybe he's not really the guy in the visions. Maybe I'm just trying to peg any guy with straight dark hair as a suicidal maniac. Maybe I should ask God to show me something a little more definite. Maybe, maybe, maybe...

By the end of the day, I think I'm probably totally wrong about Garrett. And I'm sure he must think his lab partner is one strange chick. *Stranger than he knows actually*. But I decide that whether or not Garrett Pierson is the suicidal guy in my visions, I am going to become his friend. Because I can tell he needs a friend. He's obviously lonely and a bit of a nerd. And I think it's no coincidence that I've been partnered with him. He's definitely going on my prayer list.

I convey this information to Olivia as she drives me home, but unfortunately she is still obsessing over Alex. She has now gotten it into her head that she might be able to win him back by ignoring him. I'm thinking, *Too little, too late*, but I don't say this. How can someone as intelligent as Olivia actually think that it will do any good to ignore a guy who is already ignoring you? I mean, how's he supposed to even notice?

"And," she continues, as she works through what seems to be about a ten-point plan, "I'm thinking about joining a band."

"Huh?" I turn and actually tune in to what she's saying now. "You mean like jazz band or something—"

"No, I mean a rock band."

I laugh, certain that she's pulling my leg now, which I deserve since I haven't really been listening.

"I'm serious."

"A rock band?" I study my friend. "What are you talking about?"

"Well, I guess it's not really a rock band. I think it's more alternative. That's what Cameron called it."

"Cameron Vincent?"

"Yeah. He's looking for a girl to do vocals for them. He asked me to think about auditioning."

"Are you serious?"

She gives a firm nod, but I can tell by the glint in her eyes that she's probably not as serious as she's trying to appear.

"You'd actually want to hang with *those* guys?" I imagine those hard-looking rocker dudes with their tattoos and piercings and bad boy images. Something about sweet Olivia in their midst just doesn't compute. Talk about a rose among the thorns.

"Those guys?" She glances at me as she slows down for the stop sign. "That sounds pretty judgmental, Sam."

"Well, everyone knows they're a pretty wild bunch. They're big-time partiers, and I'm pretty sure they do more than just alcohol."

She nods again. "Yes. I know that."

"You'd be comfortable with that whole scene?"

"It's not like I'd start smoking dope with them or anything."

"Well, duh."

"But maybe God is up to something."

I consider this along with my strange encounter with Garrett. "Yeah, I guess that could be. But I'd seriously pray about it first, Olivia. You don't want to get in over your head."

"I know…but I don't think it was a coincidence that Cameron brought this up to me today. It might really be a God-thing."

"That could be cool."

"Would you come with me to the audition, Sam? I mean, if I decide to go through with it?"

"Of course! And you do have a fantastic voice. Everyone knows that."

"Thanks." She's pulling up to my house now. "And one other thing."

"What?"

"Jack McAllister, you know he plays bass for the band, but he has dark brown hair—and it's straight."

"Oh?"

"Do you think?"

"I don't know…"

"Well, Jack's pretty moody. Although he was like that clear back in middle school. Of course, I've always attrib-uted that to his musician temperament and the possibility of drugs and who-knows-what. But when I was talking with Cameron and Jack about the band today, it did occur to me that Jack's just the kind of guy who could be suicidal."

"I suppose..."

"Does he look like the guy in your vision?"

I consider this. "You know there are a lot of guys who are starting to look like the guy in my vision, but I'm going to ask God to show me something a little more definite before I start putting them all on the suicide alert list."

"I'll pray too."

"Thanks." I smile at her, relieved that she seems to be coming out of her Alex funk, just a little. Maybe joining Cameron's band is just what she needs. Although I hope she's wrong about Jack. "And thanks for the ride."

She waves and drives off, and as I walk to my house, I think about all the guys with dark brown hair who could be suicidal, and it just makes me feel very, very tired. Man, it must be so hard being God—knowing all that He knows and what's going through the minds of every single person on the planet at any given time. But then I remind myself, *He IS God* after all, and He is cut out for this sort of thing.

Ten

My heart is pounding so hard that I can feel it beating against the temples of my head, and I can't seem to catch my breath. But I have to keep running. The only way out is to run for my life. Guns and bombs seem to be exploding everywhere I turn. Murderers and assassins around every corner. And the streets and the walls are varying shades of red, as if drenched in blood. I am trapped and there is no escape!

I sit up in bed and gasp. Of course, it was just a dream. Just a hideous nightmare. I wait until my breathing and heart rate return to normal, and I try to get my bearings. Finally I have to ask myself, was it just a dream? Or was it something more? It was so out of the ordinary for me—like I was trapped in some horrible video game, and I don't even play video games.

Then I realize what it was—it was *Killer7*, the same video game that Peter's little brother, Cody, was playing the day Ebony and I went to his house. I instantly recall Cody's intense face as he locked into the pretend yet violent world of that video game. Sure, it's an escape of sorts, but what a frightening one!

Feeling sorry for Cody, I pray for him, asking God to reach out to him, to give him comfort and hope. Then I go back to sleep. But the dream returns—it's the video game again, only now it features Cody, and the gun he is holding is pointed directly at me. I try to tell him to stop, to wait, to think about what he's doing, but before I can get the words out, he turns the gun to his own head—and shoots!

My heart is racing again when I wake up. It's almost six in the morning now, and although it's early, I'd rather get up than face the possibility of more dreams like these. Where are they coming from and what do they mean? Is God trying to tell me something? I write down the dream details in my notebook, then open my Bible and read today's Scripture—my way of washing away the aftermath of fear that was part of these two dreams. I pause while reading the section in Luke 14:12–14, the part where Jesus is dining with friends and everyone pushes to sit by Him. This is what Jesus tells the host of the dinner:

"The next time you put on a dinner, don't just invite your friends and family and rich neighbors, the kind of people who will return the favor. Invite some people who never get invited out, the misfits from the wrong side of the tracks. You'll be—and experience—a blessing. They won't be able to return the favor, but the favor will be returned—oh, how it will be returned!—at the resurrection of God's people."

Okay, I know *exactly* what this means, at least to me. God is trying to make me understand how important it is to reach out to people who don't exactly fit in. People like my lab partner, Garrett, or like Cameron Vincent, or the other guys in the band that Olivia is considering auditioning for. I know that God loves all those guys and wants to connect with them. I also know that God loves Cody Clark, who I'm sure is a misfit in many ways, and I believe that the dream I've just experienced is meant to be a warning for Cody's welfare. He is in danger.

Although Ebony won't be at work this early, I decide to leave a message on her voice mail anyway. I'll explain the two dreams and my concerns for Cody's safety. Although he doesn't look like the older guy in my previous suicide dreams, he definitely looked as if he could be a suicide risk himself. And really, why would that surprise anyone considering what happened to his brother? Add to that tragedy his appetite for violent video games like *Killer7*, and it seems a lethal combination.

I'm just ending my message when something new hits me. "Ebony," I say urgently, *"where was Cody when Peter shot himself?* Is it possible he was in the house at the time? I know he was probably only about seven or so, but could he have seen it happen?"

Of course, the police would probably have already questioned such an obvious possibility, but for some reason it seems important to mention this to her. Then I hang up and start getting ready for school. Cody will be in my prayers today. I'll ask Olivia to pray for him too. I really do feel he's at risk. Serious risk.

To my dismay, Garrett is not in chemistry today. Now this is actually a twofold problem: 1) I am worried about him since I still think it's possible, okay maybe even likely, that he's the guy in my suicide visions, but 2) he's the one with our chemistry notes, not to mention our brains. I am lost without him. And Mr. Dynell isn't exactly sympathetic.

"Taking the day off, Miss McGregor?" he asks when he finds me doing what I'm sure appears to be next to nothing—although in actuality I'm praying for Garrett.

"My partner's gone."

"That doesn't give you permission to daydream."

"I know."

"The project is still due on Friday."

"I know."

"Then get busy."

So I pretend to be busy but eventually decide I must be science-challenged and really need a remedial class. I do gather some statistics, which may or may not be helpful, but for the most part I'm just waiting for the bell to ring. My plan is to call Garrett and ask if he's okay. I can use chemistry as my excuse, but I really want to make sure he's still alive.

As soon as class ends, I use my cell to call information for his number. Unfortunately there are about a dozen Piersons in town, and I realize this is not going to work. Naturally, Garrett is the kind of kid with few, if any, friends and I don't have the slightest clue who I can ask for his number.

Finally, I try the counseling center. And after I explain to the receptionist that Garrett, my chemistry partner, is absent and has the notes I need if I'm going to be able to work on our project, she dials the number for me and hands me her phone. But all it does is ring and ring. No one picks up. I hand the receiver back to Mrs. Morse. "No one's home."

"Maybe he's sick in bed," she suggests.

I nod. "Yeah, maybe." Then I thank her and leave. But as soon as I'm out of the office, I call Ebony.

"I got your message," she says before I have a chance to tell her my latest concerns. "And I've been looking into it. According to our files, no one was home when Peter shot himself. But after hearing about your dreams, I'd like to question Cody when he gets home from school."

"Good." Then I tell her about Garrett. "I'm not certain that he's the guy in my suicide visions, but I'm not sure he's not." Then I explain my attempt to call and how the receptionist wouldn't give me his number. "Is there any way you can get it?"

"I'll see what I can do."

"Thanks. I'm worried about him."

"Samantha?"

I can tell by her tone that she's about to ask me a favor. "Yeah?"

"I hate to ask, but I thought it's worth a shot…would you have any interest in joining me to talk to Cody? I thought if perhaps I had you along, it would seem less intimidating, more like it's just an interview of sorts. Also, it would give you a chance to see how he reacts to my questions… in case God wants to show you something."

"Sure."

"Really?"

"Yeah, no problem."

"Great! And that brings me to something else, a little plan I've been concocting, but I'll bet I'm making you late to class."

"Actually, I've been walking toward class as we were talking, but you're right, the bell's about to ring."

"Can I pick you up after school?"

"Sure." So I hang up and get into class just as the tardy bell rings.

After school, I tell Olivia what's up. Naturally, she's curious and I fill her in on as much as I know. She, like me, has been praying for Cody today. But she didn't know that Garrett was missing in action.

"Wow, I hope he's okay."

I frown. "Me too."

"And I've set up that audition for Friday afternoon. Will you come?"

"Of course."

Then we part ways and I go out to see that Ebony is already waiting in her unmarked but fairly obvious police car. I try not to glance over my shoulder as I get in, but I do wonder what people would think if they saw me consorting with a policewoman. Hopefully I won't get a reputation for being the school nark.

"I've arranged with Mrs. Clark to speak to Cody at four," she tells me as she drives away. "Want to get a coffee first? There's something I want to talk to you about."

So we stop by Starbucks, and Ebony explains her plan. "I talked to the chief about putting you on a retainer."

"A retainer?" Okay, I'm thinking of teeth, but I've been out of braces for years now, and I don't even know what happened to my retainer.

"It's an arrangement where we would pay you for your time and assistance as a detective consultant."

I feel my eyes growing big. "A detective consultant?" That sounds so grown-up and impressive that I'm not sure how to react.

She nods but looks a little concerned. "What do you think?"

I'm not sure what to think. I can't help but feel flattered— as well as tempted. "It's interesting. I mean, on one hand I've been wanting a part-time job to earn some money, but on the other hand…" I consider what I'm about to say, not sure I want to blow off an opportunity like this so quickly.

"The other hand?"

"I don't know if it would be right. It sort of sounds like you'd be paying me to use the gift God has given me, and I think that's wrong."

"I had the same thought at first, Samantha. But I was discussing it with the chief, in all confidentiality, and as I was telling him about your ability to take the visions and dreams to the next level and actually think through and help to solve a mystery…well, it seemed like something altogether different. And I remember how you told Kayla that you were interning with us, and I just thought maybe there was a way to make this work for everyone."

"I have to admit that law enforcement has always interested me. I guess that has a lot to do with my dad. Combined with how things have gone recently."

"And you do have a gift for it. I mean beyond the gift of visions and dreams. You have an aptitude for crime solving that can't be taught."

"Thank you."

"But I can appreciate your reservations too."

I nod. "I want to respect God and His gift."

"I really do understand. And if you don't feel right about the part-time job, you might want to consider an actual internship. We can work it out with school so that you get credits for it."

"Really?"

"Of course."

"That would be awesome."

"But eventually you're going to have to answer the question about using your gift as a career too. Think about it, many people use God-given gifts in their job situations—teachers, counselors, pastors, musicians... The list could go on and on. And they all receive financial compensation for using their gifts. I don't think that makes it wrong."

"Even so, I just want to be careful, Ebony. I remember that story about the girl in Acts. She had a gift of divination, and it got her into trouble."

"I know just the story you're talking about. It's in Acts 16, and I looked it up this week because I was thinking about you and your situation. But I discovered that girl was nothing like you, Samantha. Yes, she had a gift of divining, but she was a slave and was forced to use her gift for the profit of her owners—pretty much like psychics or mediums nowadays, except for the slave part. Anyway, when she met the disciples, she discerned that they were from God and went around yelling it out and disrupting their meetings and making big scenes. They finally got fed up and rebuked her in Jesus' name, and her gift of divination went away. Of course, this ticked off her owners, and they arranged to have the disciples responsible arrested."

"Wow, I wonder what happened to the slave girl after that. Do you think they let her go free?"

Ebony laughs. "See, that's why you'd make a great detective—you're always asking the right questions."

"Because if losing her gift allowed her to go free, she might've been happier anyway. Then she could've served Jesus." I smile. "And maybe God gave her a real gift then."

Ebony nods. "I like your thinking."

"Well, I'd like to think about your offer some more," I tell her. "And I'd like to talk to my pastor about it. I've never told him what's up with all this. But he's a godly man, and I know I can trust him."

"That sounds like a wise choice."

"By the way, something occurred to me today, something that helps to convince me that Peter really wasn't the guy in my visions."

"What's that?"

"Remember the first vision I had, the jumper on the bridge?"

"Yes."

"It was totally the wrong season in my vision. The river was raging and brown, and the sky was dark and foggy."

"Not June-like weather."

"Not even close."

Ebony shakes her head. "Don't know how I missed that."

"I missed it too."

Eleven

After coffee, Ebony drives us to the Clark house. As she drives, I read over the notes about my dreams last night, just to refresh my memory. And I silently pray. I ask God to use Ebony and me—to help us help Cody.

Once again, the Clark house looks tired and worn out, sort of like someone forgot about it. And Cody looks nervous as he sits on the couch, his fingers fidgeting like he'd rather be anywhere but here. I sit with him while Ebony goes over some details with his mother. I think Mrs. Clark needs to sign a release form, and Ebony said she has the right to sit in on the interview, but she already told Ebony she'd rather not. This is hard on her.

As the two of them are quietly talking in the kitchen, I try to get Cody to open up to me a little. "You're really into video games, aren't you?"

He mumbles, "Uh-huh."

"Which is your favorite? I know you were playing *Killer7* the other day, but what other ones do you like?"

"I kinda like the *Final Fantasy* series," he says in a flat voice.

"My best friend, Olivia, likes those too," I say brightly, glad that he mentioned a game I actually recognize.

"I've only played them a few times, mostly because I'm not very good and Olivia usually cleans my clock, but the graphics on *Final Fantasy* are pretty cool."

He perks up just a little. "Does your friend have *Final Fantasy VII*?"

"I don't know. I'll have to ask her."

He picks at a hole in the knee of his jeans. "I wanna get it someday..."

"Well, if Olivia has it, maybe I can get her to loan it to you."

"Really?" He glances at me with a smidgen of interest.

"Sure. She's a really generous girl."

Now Ebony joins us. "How's it going, Cody?"

"Okay." He's back to the flat voice again and looks at her suspiciously.

"Did your mom tell you that we want to talk to you about Peter?"

He nods then looks down and starts picking at the hole again.

"I know it's been a long time since he died, Cody, but I want you to try to remember that day, okay?"

He nods very slightly, still focused on the hole in his jeans.

"According to our records you said you weren't home that day," she continues. "But we have reason to believe that might not be the truth."

He looks up with a disturbed expression. I can tell he doesn't trust us, doesn't want to have this conversation, and would probably like to bolt right now.

So I decide to jump in, hoping to reassure him. "We know there could be a reason that you didn't tell the truth," I say quietly. "I mean, I can totally understand how it feels to get really scared when someone you love is hurt like that." Then I decide to tell him a little about my dad's murder and how I actually felt somewhat responsible for his death. "It sounds sort of lame now, but at the time it seemed very real to me. I thought I was partly to blame."

Cody studies me with a creased brow. "Really? You thought it was your fault? *Why*?"

"Mostly because I was a kid. And kids usually think things are their fault. But also because I'd had this really strong feeling that something bad was going to happen to my dad, and I didn't warn him in time."

Cody nods with wide eyes, like maybe he gets this. Even so, he doesn't say anything.

"So we really need you to help us," says Ebony. "We have reason to believe that Peter didn't really kill himself that day. And we have reason to believe that you might've been home when he died. You need to tell us the truth, Cody. It's very important."

His eyes dart back and forth between Ebony and me, reminding me of a trapped animal. I don't know when I've seen such desperate fear in someone's eyes. Oh, yes, I do. It was in my dream last night, right before Cody put the revolver to his head.

"You can't make me tell you anything," he says defiantly. "Not without my lawyer present."

I sort of smile. "You have a lawyer?"

"I can get one."

Ebony nods. "Well, we don't want to arrest you, Cody. But if you refuse to tell us the truth, that could happen. And then you would need a lawyer."

His brows go up. "Really?"

"Really. But we don't think what happened to Peter was your fault—you need to understand that. We're not blaming you, and you're not a suspect."

"We just think you know something that you're not telling," I add.

"Are you afraid that something bad will happen if you tell?" asks Ebony.

Cody just looks down at his lap again. His lips are pressed tightly together, and I don't think he's going to talk.

"I had a dream about you last night, Cody," I say, unsure of how much I should disclose, but somehow I want to get through to this kid.

Fortunately, this seems to get his attention, although he looks up at me with a pretty skeptical expression. "Yeah, right."

"I really did. It was kind of weird, but in my dream you were trapped inside the *Killer7* game, and you didn't have anywhere to go."

He looks a bit stunned now. *"Really?"*

"It's the honest truth, Cody. I sometimes have strange dreams. Anyway, you seemed really scared and frantic, and I got worried that you were going to hurt yourself."

He frowns but says nothing.

"And it made me feel frightened for you. You wouldn't try to hurt yourself, would you?"

He shrugs and looks back down at his lap.

"Do you want to talk to us?" Ebony asks in a soft voice. "Tell us what happened that day?"

He says nothing.

"We only want to help you," I add.

"But we can't help you if you don't talk."

He looks at Ebony with a hardened expression. "I'm not talking to no one." Then he stands and backs away from us. "You can't make me."

"The court can make you," Ebony says in a firmer tone. "But we'd rather not do it like that."

"You better talk to my lawyer first," he says in a gruff voice, like he's really not just twelve years old. "I got nothing to say to nobody."

Ebony nods. "I'm sorry about that, Cody."

Then he turns and stomps out of the room. I look at Ebony, but she actually seems okay. However, this did not go the way I'd hoped. Now I feel even more concerned about this troubled boy. If he had problems before, he probably really feels like he's got them now. We talk briefly to Cody's mom. Ebony tells her to keep an eye on the boy, that Cody might be rattled by this conversation.

"Call me if he decides he wants to talk." She hands Mrs. Clark a business card. "Or if anything new develops."

Then we leave. But I feel so bad for Cody. I almost wish I hadn't come with Ebony.

"How is it going to help anything to have Cody so upset by this?" I ask once we're in the car.

"I know it's hard. But sometimes witnesses have to get rattled in order to talk. And I have no doubt now that I've seen his reaction. Cody does know something about his brother's death."

"Why won't he talk?"

"He's obviously frightened."

"Of what?" I ask, although I have my own suspicions.

"I figure it could be several possibilities. One, the most obvious is that Cody saw his brother shoot himself. If that's the case, we can close this thing down for good. But I don't think that's what happened. Two, and I don't think this is very likely either, but Cody might've been involved in the shooting. Maybe he got the gun from his father's drawer, and maybe it accidentally went off, hitting his brother in the head, and he stuck it in Peter's hand to look like a suicide. But that wouldn't explain the suicide note."

The thought of this makes me feel sick. "That would be so awful. For Cody's sake I hope that theory's wrong. What a horrible load for a boy to carry."

"Well, I don't really think that's what happened."

"So what do you think did happen?"

"I think Cody witnessed his brother's murder. It was prob-ably someone involved in the drugs. Maybe that so-called best friend, Brett Carnes. Or maybe even the girlfriend, Faith Mitchell, although that wouldn't explain her e-mail."

"Unless she was feeling guilty," I say, "and wanted Peter's mother to know that Peter didn't kill himself."

"Yes, that's possible. But it still doesn't explain the suicide note."

"Unless…" I suddenly remember something.

"Unless?"

"Unless the suicide note *wasn't* written by Peter. Remember how Olivia and I registered on the suicide website, using fake names? Isn't it possible that someone else, maybe even Brett or the girlfriend, could have registered on the site using Peter's name?"

"You could be on to something," Ebony says as she turns down a street that's unfamiliar.

"Where are you going?"

"Didn't you want to pay a visit to your friend Garrett Pierson?"

"You mean go up to his house and knock on the door—straight out of the blue?"

"I suppose you could call first."

Then she gives me the number and I call. But once again, no one answers. "Maybe we should go to his house. I can always pretend that I came to pick up the chemistry notes. I actually do need them if he's not going to be in school tomorrow. I can tell him that I assumed he was sick."

"Sounds like a plan." She pulls up in front of a house that reminds me of our house. Not fancy, but nice, and certainly not as run-down as the Clark house. "I'll wait here."

"Thanks." I feel nervous as I walk toward the house. I'm still constructing what I'll say to him as I ring the doorbell. That is if he answers, which I seriously doubt.

Even so, I feel determined to try. I want to establish that Garrett is really okay and that he hasn't taken his life. I ring the doorbell again. Then to my surprise the door opens, just a few inches.

"Samantha?"

"Garrett, you're home!"

"What do you want?"

"I've been trying to call you. I need to get the chemistry notes. Mr. Dynell got on my case today. And if you're sick, I'll really need them for tomorrow."

The door opens a bit wider, just wide enough to see part of his face, but it's dimly lit in there and I can barely make out his features. "I'll e-mail them to you."

"Oh, okay. Are you sick?"

"Yeah."

"Sorry to bother you," I say. "But I really did miss you in chemistry today."

"Sorry."

"Will you be gone tomorrow too?"

He clears his throat. "I don't know."

"But you'll send me the notes?"

"Yeah."

"Okay, then, take care, Garrett. I hope you feel better soon."

"Thanks."

I hear the door click shut as I turn to walk back to the car, but I have a feeling he's watching me from inside. I hope he bought my story. I think it was pretty believable. And I hope he's really okay.

"How'd it go?" asks Ebony.

"All right, I guess. I mean, he was there. He hasn't killed himself or anything."

She shakes her head. "This gets a little depressing, doesn't it? We interview one family who is, after five years, still recovering from an alleged suicide, and on top of that you get to worry about your friend doing the same thing himself."

"Yeah, it's kind of a bummer."

"But do you think he's okay?"

"It's hard to say. But he did promise to e-mail me the notes for chemistry, and I'm thinking it might be my way to get to know him better, you know, by e-mailing him back. This kid seems pretty shy when we're talking face-to-face."

"Sounds smart. I'll be praying for him, Samantha. And for you too."

After Ebony drops me home, I call our church and make an appointment with Pastor Ken. His secretary, Myrna Glass, sounds cheerful but curious. I haven't been in for a counseling session for several years now. When I came a few years ago, it was mostly to help me deal with my dad's death from a Christian perspective. My mom's counseling friend, Paula Stone, the one who thought I was slightly nuts because of "seeing things," never gave me much support on a spiritual level. But Pastor Ken has been encouraging.

"I just need to ask him some advice about something," I tell her. Not that she needs to know everything, but I figure it can't hurt to assure her that nothing serious is wrong with me. I'm sure they get plenty of that.

"Well, Pastor Ken is a good one for giving advice," she says. "How does Thursday afternoon at four sound?"

"Sounds perfect."

As I hang up, I realize that this presents a small problem. I'll need to tell Pastor Ken about my gift now, and it's something I don't really like to disclose. Of course, being a pastor, he's used to keeping people's secrets, and I'm sure he respects confidentiality. But I also know that life could get difficult for me if word of this leaked out into the congregation. What if people started asking me to find things out for them? That could get seriously twisted.

Anyway, I'll share my anonymity concerns with him, as well as my concern about working for the police department and getting paid for it. The problem is that I'm afraid I'm not exactly neutral about this.

The truth is, I really would love to work for the police department. I find it exciting and fulfilling, like it's something God has made me good at. And the possibility of being paid for helping Ebony on cases is way cool. But what if it's wrong? What if God has a different plan for me?

Twelve

True to his word, Garrett e-mails me the chemistry notes, and I e-mail him back, asking if this means he doesn't plan on being at school tomorrow. I figure this is a pretty natural question since he is my lab partner.

I wait a few minutes after e-mailing him, but he doesn't e-mail back right away, so I decide to check out the suicide website. Like I need more depressing stuff. Or maybe I'm just curious as to the status of the death wish crowd. But to my surprise there is one positive response to the e-mails that Olivia and I sent on my birthday.

To Hope and Grace,

Thank you for writing your thoughts about suicide on this website. You've made me reconsider some things, and today I went to a counselor and told her what I'd been planning. I can't promise that I won't kill myself, but I will carefully think about it first. You made me see that suicide really is a final act, and unless I really know what comes next, it IS pretty risky.

Still here, Becca

This is so exciting that I copy it and paste Becca's post in an e-mail to Olivia. Since she'd been as bummed as I was when she read the negative responses we'd gotten, I'm sure she'll be glad to hear that someone was listening. I'm also pretty sure she hasn't gone back to check it out since then either.

I decide to read more of the e-mails. I'm thinking about Peter and how he supposedly participated in that site before killing himself. But more than ever, I'm convinced that's not the case. After seeing Cody's reaction to Ebony's questions, I have to agree with her that someone else was involved. Someone who faked Peter's identity on this very website. Someone who I believe was intent on carrying out a well-planned and premeditated murder. Of course, I have no idea why that would be. I do know drugs were involved somehow, and I know, because of my own brother's various drug-related dilemmas, that it can really complicate everything.

As I'm spacing out, pondering the possibilities of Peter's death, I notice a new message pop up on the suicide site. The name of the writer is slightly familiar from the last time I was visiting. As I recall, he goes by "gay guy" or "gg," and his main excuse for wanting to check out is because he can't deal with being gay— it's too hard. Somehow his homophobic dad found out a few weeks ago, and he's been making gg's life miserable ever since. Pretty sad. I wonder why the mom doesn't intervene.

to whom it may concern—yeah, sure.

I don't know why I keep putting this off.
Things are definitely not getting better. My
dad, the big macho man, put away about a case
of beer last night and then decided to see if he
could "knock the gay outta me." Life stinks.
After much careful thought and consideration,
I've decided there's no perfect way to exit this
messed-up planet. The easiest way is probably
carbon monoxide poisoning, but that's only easy
if you have access to a car, which I do not
since my dad doesn't trust me. He keeps his
pickup keys with him 24-7, even when drunk.
Maybe I'll just do the military thing—and
down a bottle of Tylenol. Although I don't
like the idea of being around for a day or two
before my liver shuts down, and I know from
research that lingering is a real possibility with
acetaminophen poisoning. The upside is that I
might get to see my dad feeling guilty while
I'm fighting it out in the ER. Nah, I doubt
that. He'd probably be the one to pull the
plug on my life-support system. Any new ideas
out there? I wish I wasn't afraid of heights—
that would be quick and easy. Help
appreciated.

JJ

Before I can even think about it, I decide to write this poor guy back. Maybe he's just trying to get attention, but he sounds truly desperate—way more than the last time I read one of his posts. And he's right—he does need help. And not just a new recipe for suicide either.

> Dear gg,
>
> Your dad is a total jerk. And just because he's a jerk doesn't mean you should give up on your life. Do you realize that if you give up, your dad, the jerk, wins? And why would you want to let a jerk beat you out of your own life? Please consider seeing a counselor. Being gay is not a death sentence. Your cry for help was the only thing you got right. You DO need help. Please, get some ASAP.
>
> Praying for you, Grace

I've just hit Send when my cell phone rings. I figure it's either Ebony or Olivia, since they're the only ones who use this number. It turns out to be Olivia.

"Are you home yet?"

"Yeah, what's up?"

"Well, after you skipped out on the Honor Society meeting after school, I actually went to it and got roped into heading up the decorating committee for the Sweethearts Ball."

I laugh. "For Valentine's Day?"

"Yeah. Ironic, isn't it?"

"Actually, it's great. You'll be really good at decorations." I don't add that this might also help to keep her mind off Alex.

"Well, I signed you up too."

"Olivia!"

"Come on, I need some help, Sam. Nobody *wants* to do this. I was actually trying to slip out the back door when Emma Piscolli nominated me."

"Why didn't you nominate Emma right back?"

"I did, but they put it to a vote and I won."

"Lucky you. Congratulations."

"Thanks a lot. And now you *have* to help me, okay?"

"All right," I agree. "It might actually be a nice change of pace."

"You mean as compared to working on gruesome things like murders, suicides, and kidnappings?"

"Olivia!" I use a warning tone. "Is anyone listening to you?"

"I'm in my car. Chill."

"Okay." Then I tell her about the response we got from Becca on the suicide website. "I e-mailed it to you. It's enough to give a person hope."

"Well, I better hang up and head for home now. I just wanted to make sure I had your support for the decorations."

I make a dramatic groan. "But let's keep it simple, okay?"

"Exactly."

"And let's recruit more helpers. How about if we get some of the sophomores who got inducted last spring?"

"Good idea. They have to do what we tell them to."

"If it wasn't basketball season, I'd try to get Conrad to help."

"And if Alex hadn't—"

"Don't go there, Olivia," I say quickly. Then we hang up. Good for Olivia. At least she's out there doing something different. First she's auditioning with Cameron Vincent's band, which I remind myself is on Friday, and now she's heading up the decorations committee for the dance. I have to hand it to her.

I'm about to turn off my computer when I notice that Garrett has replied to my e-mail. Eager to see how he's doing, I open it.

Hi Sam (is it okay if I call you that since you signed your e-mail with it?). I'm not sure if I'll be in school tomorrow. I think I have the flu. But now that you have the notes, you should be okay in chemistry. The actual experiment isn't until Friday, and I'll try to be there by then. In the meantime, you better pay attention and take good notes. No more riding on my coattails.

later, garrett

I decide to write back. Maybe I can draw him out some more. I don't want to lead him on exactly, but it's okay for him to know that I think he's a nice guy.

Sorry you have the flu. I hope you're not feeling too yucky. Would you like me to stop by any of your classes to pick up homework for you? I hope I can hold chemistry together until the end of the week. I'll send you my notes after school tomorrow, that is if I have any. Then maybe you can have things ready by Friday. I am lost without you in that class, Garrett. I hope you know that. And I actually miss you too. You're a cool guy. And I hope you feel better soon.

Take care, Sam

I hit Send and wait a few minutes, thinking maybe he's still online. Maybe he'll write back and I can continue the conversation. But there is nothing. And for some reason this worries me. So I get another idea and send him a message titled "PS."

Oh, yeah, I forgot to ask you if you're okay being on the decorating committee for the Sweethearts Ball. You obviously weren't at the Honor Society meeting today, and since Olivia Marsh is heading up the decorations committee, I thought you might like to join us in cutting out hearts and things.

Thanks so much! Sam

I chuckle as I hit Send. Talk about roping somebody into something. And my trick works, because now I get a reply.

I'm not making any promises about the
decorating committee. But if it works out,
I suppose I could lend a hand. But be warned,
we science geeks are not very artsy-fartsy.

later, garrett

His little joke seems like an invitation to e-mail back. And we actually go back and forth a few times. And by the time I sign off for good, I'm feeling hopeful. Maybe Garrett really isn't the guy in my visions. Maybe he's just a frustrated science geek who needs a friend. I'll keep praying for him.

The next day, I'm not terribly surprised that Garrett's not at school. But I seriously miss him in chemistry. Even so, I try to take notes and make some calculations and predictions and things. Still, I'm in over my head. Way over my head. After school, Olivia takes me to the church for my little "counseling session" with Pastor Ken. Of course, she knows what's up and doesn't mind waiting for me. Especially since I promised to accompany her to the craft store when we're done—to shop for decorations for the dance.

"So what brings you here today?" Pastor Ken finally asks me after a couple minutes of obvious small talk.

I suppress a fluttery feeling of nervousness and attempt to begin what turns out to be a fairly lengthy explanation of my gift and how my dad recognized it early on, how my grandmother had the same gift, and how I've recently put it to use with Ebony on the police force. And by the time I'm done, Pastor Ken has a slightly stunned look on his face. I'm not sure he's even taking me seriously.

"I know this must all sound pretty strange," I say quickly. "But I'm not making it up."

He shakes his head. "No, I don't think you're making it up, Samantha. It's just that in all my years of counseling members of the congregation, well, I've never run into anything like this."

"Does it bother you?" Okay, I'm feeling a little defensive now. Like what is he saying? Am I some sort of spiritual misfit? Does he think my gift is bogus? Or that it's not of God?

He smiles. "No, it doesn't bother me. But I'm at a bit of a loss for words at the moment." He reaches for his Bible now. "Do you mind if I read some Scripture to you? And to me?"

"No, of course not."

He flips through the thin pages. "This is from the Gospel of John, chapter 16." He clears his throat and reads.

"'When the Friend comes, the Spirit of the Truth, he will take you by the hand and guide you into all the truth there is. He won't draw attention to himself, but will make sense out of what is about to happen and, indeed, out of all that I have done and said. He will honor me; he will take from me and deliver it to you. Everything the

Father has is also mine. That is why I've said, "He takes from me and delivers to you." In a day or so you're not going to see me, but then in another day or so you will see me."'

He looks up at me. "Do you know what that's about, Samantha?"

"The Holy Spirit?" I venture hopefully.

He smiles. "That's right. Shortly before the Crucifixion, Jesus was talking about how the Holy Spirit would come to us and say things and show us things. Scripture also speaks of other gifts that will come through the Holy Spirit, some that are unexplainable and unimaginable. But if they are from God, they bring glory to Him."

I consider this. "Do you think my gift is from God?"

"What do you think?"

"I think it is."

"What makes you think that?" He's leaning forward as if my answer really interests him.

"Partly because of the way it comes to me. It's so out of the blue, and it just feels like God to me. But then it's always about helping someone who's in a tough situation. And it makes me really care about people—sometimes people that I would've otherwise ignored. And then I begin to pray for them, and it makes me want to help them in whatever way I can. That seems like God to me."

He smiles. "Yes, it seems like God to me too, Samantha."

Then I tell him about how I keep this thing secret, how it seems important to remain as anonymous as possible.

"That must be tricky when you're assisting the police."

"I work primarily with one detective, Ebony Hamilton. She used to be my dad's partner."

He nods. "Yes, I've met her before. Fine woman."

So then I tell him about Ebony's job proposition to me. And he listens carefully. "But I just wasn't sure," I finally say. "I wondered if it was wrong to receive money for using my God-given gift."

"Do you think it's wrong?"

"I'm not sure. I don't want to misuse or abuse it. I'm pretty sure God would take it away from me if I did." Then I tell him about the brief period of quiet, after telling God I needed a break during the holidays, and how worried it got me.

"I mean, if God decided it wasn't good to give me this gift, I guess I'd have to understand and accept it. And I know He'd still talk to me in other ways. But I want to be careful with it. If it's wrong to be paid, I don't want to be paid. But I just don't know. That's why I wanted to talk to you, Pastor Ken. Ebony thought it was a good idea too."

"Well, as you know, many of God's servants are paid for using their gifts. Take me, for instance, I have a gift of pastoring, teaching, counseling…and I am on salary at the church."

"I know."

"And there are people who are gifted in music, and many of them receive payment for those gifts."

"I know that too."

And he goes on and on, mentioning all kinds of people who are involved in ministries and things—all who receive money for it. "Do you think that invalidates their gifts? Does that make it wrong?"

"I guess not."

"As in all things, you need to search your own heart and listen to that still, small voice of the Holy Spirit, Samantha. I'm sure there are some instances when it would be wrong to take payment for a God-given gift. For instance, I would never allow anyone to pay me for praying for them. That would be wrong."

"I saw a TV evangelist doing that once," I point out. "But I thought it was wrong."

He holds up his hands. "And yet I don't think I'd want to be the judge of others."

I consider this. "I guess I wouldn't either. But I still think it's tacky."

He laughs and winks at me. "I do too."

There's a brief silence now, and I wonder if we're done here.

"Do you know what you want to do after high school? Do you have a career direction yet? A college picked out?"

So I tell him about my love of law enforcement and crime solving, and he nods and smiles. "Then it seems to make perfect sense. God has given you a very special gift, Samantha, and it seems He wants you to use it. It also seems a bit ridiculous to think of you working for free."

I brighten. "So you think it's okay?"

"I think it's okay. But it's more important that you believe *God* is telling you it's okay. It's good to seek counsel and advice, but it's just as important to hear what God is telling you." Then he jots something down on a slip of paper and slides it across the table. "Read these Scriptures tonight."

"Okay."

"And keep me informed of what's going on," he says. "This is very interesting to me. In fact, I'd love to discuss it with Ebony Hamilton."

"I'll let her know."

"And you can trust your secret with me, Samantha."

I smile. "I thought so."

"One small word of caution to you though."

"What's that?"

"So much of life is about balance, Samantha. I think I appreciate that more the older I get. As your pastor and friend, I encourage you to maintain balance in your life."

"What do you mean exactly?"

"Well, you're a teenage girl. And you'll only be a teenage girl once in your lifetime. It's a delightful time for all sorts of delightful things. And I'd hate to see you getting so bogged down in the heavy world of crime and such…so much so that you miss out on some other more frivolous things. I do believe that God wants you to enjoy your youth too. So to do that and keep balance, I think you'll have to lean heavily on God."

I nod. "Yes, I think you're right. And I do try to lean on Him."

"Good." He shakes my hand and reminds me to stay in touch. And I feel as if a load's been lifted as I rejoin Olivia where she's been waiting outside his office.

"Everything go okay?" she asks hopefully.

So I tell her about our conversation as she drives us to Craft World to shop for the dance decorations. We have a budget of one hundred dollars to get everything we need to make the cafeteria look like a romantic setting for a Sweethearts Ball. I tell her I'm imagining lots of pink and red crepe paper and maybe some goofy-looking cupids slapped on the walls.

Of course, Olivia says that'll look like a kindergarten project. I'm thinking I don't really care. Mostly I can't wait to call Ebony and tell her the good news! Well, after I read whatever it is that Pastor Ken wrote down. Hopefully it won't change anything.

Thirteen

Who's going to blow up all those balloons?"
I ask when Olivia and I are finally done with our mad hunt
for Valentine's decorations. The lesson to be learned here
is that you shouldn't wait until a week before Valentine's
Day to shop for decorations. It's taken four different stores
and three and a half hours, including a short dinner break,
but I think we've got it bagged. We better since we ran out
of money about thirty bucks ago. Olivia chipped in.

"We'll get the sophomores to do the balloons," she
says as she backs out of the parking spot. "They're probably full of hot air."

"How about some hot air in here." I rub my hands
together. It's been raining like crazy all night long, and it
feels like I'm soaked clear through.

"I hope we got enough balloons." Olivia turns up the
heat as she drives through a puddle that shoots out on
both sides.

"I think you got every red, pink, and white balloon in
town. What're we going to do with all of them anyway?"

"We'll make an archway shaped like a heart to be set
by the entrance. Couples can get their pictures taken in it.
Kind of like prom."

"Only cheesier," I add. "If that's even possible." Okay, neither of us actually went to the prom last year, but we heard it was pretty lame, with their "space age" theme. Kind of like a kiddie birthday party.

"For a smart girl, you sometimes lack imagination, Sam."

Of course, I know what she means by this. She's implying that my imagination works great when I'm dealing with things like unsolved crimes, but when it comes to balloons and crepe paper, I'm pretty hopeless.

"Do you think I'm unbalanced?" I suddenly ask.

"What?" She glances at me then back to the wet black road. "You mean as in unstable? Crazy? Bonkers?"

"Unbalanced as a person, like I focus too much on heavy stuff like solving crimes."

"Did Pastor Ken say something to make you think that?"

"Not exactly. He just warned me to be careful and to remember to be a regular teenage girl and have fun. So tell me the truth: Do you think I'm at risk here? Am I unbalanced?"

She seems to consider this. "Well, I think it could happen... I mean, the crud you work with is pretty serious. And sometimes I've seen you get a little down when you can't resolve something. But you have great resiliency, Sam. You seem to do really well at bouncing back. In fact, I've been trying to learn from you lately."

"You mean in regard to recovering from Alex?"

"Recovering from Alex." She kind of laughs. "Sounds like the title of a movie. And it probably seems silly since we weren't really a couple. But I've had a crush on him for so long, and I'd hoped..."

"I know…" I hope we're not going to digress here.

"Anyway, if you haven't noticed, I've been trying to keep a sunny disposition lately. But it's not easy. Still, it's a lot better when I keep myself busy and focused on other things. You were right about that. I guess I need to be more balanced too."

"Well, I give you permission to let me know if I ever seem out of balance."

"It's a deal," she tells me. "You better do the same thing for me."

When I get home, I go straight to my computer to e-mail Garrett with today's chemistry junk. I so need his help if I'm going to make it through this class. If not, I better drop it in time to pick up another credit, even if it's just a pottery class.

I hit Send and wait for him to reply. Like I think he's just sitting there waiting for my message. But after about ten minutes I realize that's probably not the case. Even a science geek might have a life. Hopefully he's feeling better by now.

"Did you and Olivia get everything for the dance?" Mom asks as she pokes her head in my room. I called her earlier to explain why I'd be home late tonight.

"I guess so." Then I tell her about Olivia's heart-shaped archway plan and the millions of balloons required to create it.

"Sounds like fun." Mom smiles. "Are you going to the dance with Conrad?"

"Well, he hasn't exactly asked me yet. He's so busy with basketball…but I assume he will."

"I remember a Valentine's dance when I was your age," she says wistfully. "All I wanted was for Brad Miller to ask me. I dreamed about it, planned it, strategized, and eventually I got my best friend, Bonnie, to drop lots of hints. I even had a dress all ready for the big night. It was hot pink satin and white lace with these big shoulder pads." She laughs. "I'm sure it would look just hideous nowadays."

"So did Brad ask you to the dance?"

She folds her arms across her chest and shakes her head. "I really thought he was going to. Right up until a couple of days beforehand. But he asked Bonnie instead—apparently she did more hinting for herself than she did for me."

"Seriously? Did she really go with him?"

Mom nods. "She sure did."

"Was she still your best friend after that?"

Mom chuckles. "Not for a few days."

"So did you even get to go to the dance?"

"Actually, I did."

"Who asked you?"

She looks slightly embarrassed. "The truth is I asked him."

"Who?"

"Your dad." She tosses me a smirky smile.

"No way!"

Mom starts laughing. "It's true. I was the first one to break the ice between us. He was a senior, I was a junior, and he was awfully shy, but I thought he seemed nice. I had geometry with him. And I thought, *What the heck? Why not?*"

"So did you guys start dating regularly after that?"

"It was sort of off and on. It wasn't until he went away to college the next fall that he really started thinking about me. We started writing letters, and by Christmas we were going steady."

"That's so sweet," I tell her. "I never even knew that before."

Mom grins. "See, I had a few tricks up my sleeve."

"By the way, are we still going shopping on Saturday?" I ask, almost afraid that she might've forgotten our plans.

She nods. "I told them I wasn't coming in on Saturdays anymore—not unless there's an emergency."

"Good for you."

"Well, I won't keep you. I know you're busy." Just as she says this, I notice an e-mail from Garrett has popped onto my screen.

I start to tell her that it's okay and I'm not busy, but she's already heading for her room. So I open Garrett's post, relieved that he's written back.

Sam,

Guess I'll be in school tomorrow after all. Not that I'm feeling all that great. See you in chem.

garrett

Not terribly encouraging, but at least he'll be in school. I decide to write back, something that I hope will be uplifting to him. His brief message makes me think he's still feeling bummed about something.

Hey, Garrett!

Glad you're feeling well enough to go to school tomorrow. I really need you in chem class—I'm not kidding; today felt like drowning. I couldn't keep my head above water. Anyway, I hope you'll feel even better by morning. Be sure and drink lots of fluids tonight. My mom swears green tea is really good when you're sick. BTW, Olivia and I got lots of decorations for the dance tonight. We're counting on your help. We won't start until Monday because Olivia is auditioning Friday for Cameron Vincent's band—if you can believe that! I'll fill you in later. But having the whole weekend to rest up should give you plenty of time to get totally over the flu so you can help us on Monday. Right? See ya tomorrow.

Your friend, Sam

Okay, I hope I didn't push things too far. I don't want to scare him, or cause him to read more into it than I meant to say. But I do want him to know that I'm sincere and that I want to be his friend. I wait a few minutes and am not too surprised when he doesn't write back. So I decide to zero in on my homework.

Finally, it's late and although I still have a half-finished writing project, I feel certain I can get it done in the morning. But before going to bed, I pull out the slip of paper that

Pastor Ken gave to me. It says, 1 Corinthians 2:9–16. It's a fairly long section, so I decide to read it in bed. I hope I don't fall asleep before I finish it.

"No one's ever seen or heard anything like this,

Never so much as imagined anything quite like it—

What God has arranged for those who love him."

But you've seen and heard it because God by his Spirit has brought it all out into the open before you.

The Spirit, not content to flit around on the surface, dives into the depths of God, and brings out what God planned all along. Who ever knows what you're thinking and planning except you yourself? The same with God—except that he not only knows what he's thinking, but he lets us in on it. God offers a full report on the gifts of life and salvation that he is giving us. We don't have to rely on the world's guesses and opinions. We didn't learn this by reading books or going to school; we learned it from God, who taught us person-to-person through Jesus, and we're passing it on to you in the same firsthand, personal way.

The unspiritual self, just as it is by

nature, can't receive the gifts of God's Spirit. There's no capacity for them. They seem like so much silliness. Spirit can be known only by spirit—God's Spirit and our spirits in open communion. Spiritually alive, we have access to everything God's Spirit is doing, and can't be judged by unspiritual critics. Isaiah's question, "Is there anyone around who knows God's Spirit, anyone who knows what he is doing?" has been answered: Christ knows, and we have Christ's Spirit.

Wow, that is good. Really, really excellent. And so awesomely fitted to my life that even though it's late and I'm tired, I read it all over again. Then I put a marker in my Bible and decide I will read it a few more times and copy it into my journal. It's a lot to take in, but it seems to make sense. And it's encouraging. "Spiritually alive." That sounds so right. And that's how I feel: The more I tune in to God, the more *spiritually alive* I become. I wish everyone could feel this alive.

Fourteen

Today's the big day," Olivia says in an unenthusiastic voice. She's driving us to school, and something seems to be bugging her.

"Huh?"

"My audition. Remember?"

"Oh, yeah."

"You're still coming, aren't you?"

"Of course."

"I was actually considering chickening out."

"Why?"

"Oh, I don't know…"

"Just second thoughts?"

"Yeah. If you think about it, it's pretty wild."

"I felt like that too at first, but I liked your initial reasoning about this whole thing, Olivia, the way you wanted to reach out to these guys. I think that's cool. And I plan to be praying for you and for them while you're auditioning."

"So you really think I should go through with it?"

"Yeah. Put it in God's hands. If He has a reason for you to hang with these guys, He'll work it out. Otherwise, let's just pray that they reject you."

She laughs. "I guess that will help me to feel better if they do."

"What are they called anyway?"

"Stewed Oysters."

"Right." I wonder if there's something metaphorical about that or if they just liked the sound of it. Band names are always so bizarre.

I stay on the lookout for Conrad today. I realize how little we've talked this week and feel slightly concerned. Also, I'm hoping that I can gently hint that he should invite me to next week's dance. But the only time I see him in the morning is just before third period, and he seems preoccupied. He just waves and says he'll catch me later. And then he's not anywhere to be found during lunch. As I'm going to chemistry, I finally spot Alex and ask him if everything's okay with Conrad.

"He's just stressing over tonight's game."

"With McKinley High?"

"Yeah, they were last year's state champs, and Coach Keller has really been on the team's case this week." Alex laughs. "Like Brighton has a chance at state. Yeah, right."

"So that's all?"

Alex shrugs. "That's all I know." Now he glances around, like he's making sure no one is listening. "I feel kinda bad about Olivia, you know. Is she okay and everything?"

I smile. "She's doing great. Did you know she's trying out for Cameron Vincent's band?"

He frowns. "Are you kidding?"

"Totally serious."

"Olivia in that band—what're they called anyway? Oyster Stew?"

"Stewed Oysters."

"Whatever." He lowers his voice now. "But everyone knows they're a bunch of dopers."

I force a smile. "Jesus loves dopers too. Not that I know they are. To be honest, I was a little worried at first. But Olivia knows what she's doing."

He rolls his eyes. "Sounds pretty weird to me."

Just then I see Garrett, although he looks rather un-Garrett-like, wearing a pair of wire-rimmed sunglasses. "See ya later," I call as I dash off to catch up with him. It's funny that Alex seems so concerned about Olivia getting involved with this band. Go figure.

"Hey, Garrett," I say as I join him. "How's it going?"

"Okay," he mumbles.

"What's up with the shades? Trying to keep a low profile so the paparazzi won't mob you?"

"Funny."

"Sorry." I glance at him. "Are you feeling better?"

"I guess."

Then we're in chemistry, and Garrett is all business. He's logging things into his laptop and getting stuff ready for our experiment, and I'm like his dumb assistant, following orders and cracking jokes that he doesn't even smile at. All the while he keeps his sunglasses on. Weird.

Finally, we're done and Mr. Dynell seems pleased with our results. I watch as Garrett logs more statistics into his computer. Then I notice something as I catch him from a side angle.

"Do you have a black eye?" I point to his right eye, and he turns away. "You do, don't you? What happened? Did you get into a fight?"

"Yeah," he says dryly. "A fight with a door. I got up in the middle of the night when I was sick and ran smack into the bathroom door."

"Ouch."

He nods. "A rude awakening."

"Looks like it got your nose too." I notice what I can now see is some swelling. "That must've hurt."

"Uh-huh." He closes his laptop and looks at me like he's trying to figure out who I really am and what I'm up to.

"What's wrong?"

"Just wondering."

"What?"

"Why are you being so nice to me?"

I smile. "Why not?"

"Well, I know you need my help in this class. But something else is going on too."

I give him an innocent look. "I just happen to like you, Garrett. You're a nice guy. And I appreciate that you're smart. I think you'd be a good friend."

"You mean you think I could use a friend?"

"Whatever."

"Am I some sort of mission for you? A let's-make-a-friend charity case?"

"Of course, not."

"What then?"

"I don't see why you're such a skeptic."

"I'm scientific. It's my nature."

I laugh. "You've actually got a pretty good sense of humor."

"Thanks a lot." But his expression is still glum.

"And you seem a little down to me. I could be wrong. Maybe it was just the flu. But I guess I thought you could use a friend. And why shouldn't we be friends?"

He shrugs.

"And we do need help for the Sweethearts Ball."

He lets out an exasperated sigh. "So that's it?"

"No, that's not it. I got dragged into it by Olivia, and now I'm dragging you into it too. But you are on Honor Society, so you really do have a responsibility to do your—"

"Yeah, yeah." He seems to loosen up. "So, what's the deal with Olivia trying out for Stewed Oysters? That seems a little off-the-wall, if you ask me."

"Yeah, it's kinda weird. But Olivia has a really good voice and she does play several instruments, and they needed a female vocalist, so she thought, why not?"

He shakes his head like he's trying to imagine it.

"Sometimes we need to try something new." I grin at him. "Like new friends. It makes life interesting." Then I get an idea, and without fully thinking it through, I decide to go for it. "Hey, why don't you come with us?"

"Huh?"

"To the audition. I'm going to sort of support Olivia. You could come along and just watch. Do you like music?"

"Well, yeah, who doesn't like music?"

"How about Stewed Oysters? Have you heard them before?"

"Yeah. They were pretty good at Battle of the Bands last spring."

"Well, then come with us."

"Are you serious?"

"Definitely. Come on, Garrett."

He sort of shrugs. "Well, okay, I guess I—"

"Good. Meet us by the west exit after school, okay?"

"Yeah, I guess."

Then class is over, and I tell Garrett good-bye and that I'll see him later. Okay, I'm not totally sure that he'll show up or what Olivia will think, but I have a feeling she'll be all right with it.

I catch her on the way to my next class and give her a heads-up about inviting Garrett. At first she's surprised, but then she's fine. "The more the merrier."

"Thanks," I tell her. "I just think Garrett needs some friends right now."

"Do you still think he's the suicide guy in your visions?"

"Not really. But I do think he's lonely. And he's actually kinda fun. For an academic, he's got a pretty good sense of humor."

"See ya after school, Sam."

Then as I'm on my way to art, my last class, my cell phone rings. Assuming it must be Ebony and hoping that nothing's gone wrong with Cody, since he's been on my heart today, I immediately answer.

"Hey, I heard the fantastic news," says Ebony. "And I'm so excited!"

"Oh, that's right. I almost forgot that I left you a message this morning."

"So your pastor was really okay about you working for us?"

"He was totally great! It was actually a huge relief to tell him about the whole thing. He's a very cool guy."

"I know. I've met him before. He seemed very well grounded and genuine."

"And he wants to talk to you. I told him I'd let you know."

"I'll give him a call."

"Any word on Cody? Did his mom call or anything? I've been thinking about him a lot today." I lower my voice. "But no visions or dreams or anything."

"I haven't heard a thing."

I sigh. "Too bad, I've really been praying for him to open up to someone. That's a heavy load for a twelve-year-old to carry."

"I feel exactly the same way. And I sure don't want to request a court order to bring him in here. I told his mom that I'm giving Cody until next week to come forward."

"I'll keep praying for him. In the meantime I better get to class."

"Yes, of course. Let's plan on getting together on Monday after school, Samantha. You'll need to sign some paperwork here, things to make your employment official."

"Cool."

"I'm heading off to a wedding this weekend. But if anything new comes up, feel free to call. Not that I'll be much help out in Des Moines, but I can probably find someone else to step in."

"Have a great weekend," I tell her. "I'll see you on Monday."

Finally, the day ends and I'm heading to the west exit to meet Olivia. I'm almost there when I notice Garrett sort of meandering that way too, like maybe his enthusiasm is lagging a little and he may need a boost, so I come up from behind and grab him by the arm. Of course, this just makes him jump.

"Sorry," I say, still linked arm in arm with him. "Didn't mean to scare you. Ready to go to Olivia's audition?"

"I don't know if that's—"

"Come on, Garrett. It'll be fun. And I already told Olivia you were coming. She's expecting you."

Garrett looks unsure, but I just keep escorting him toward the exit. It's a good thing he's not a real big guy since I can tell he's dragging his heels a little. But I also hope that maybe he's enjoying the attention. I sense that we're being observed, and I'm sure people wonder what's up with me and Garrett. But I don't really care. If anything, I'm sure we make a pretty funny pair.

"Hey," calls Olivia. "Ready to go?"

"Your fan club has arrived," I tell her.

"Hey, Garrett," she says with a big, beautiful Olivia smile, which actually seems to dazzle him just slightly. I'm sure he's not at all used to getting this kind of attention from girls. "Nice shades."

"Thanks," he says quietly.

She jingles her car keys. "Let's go, kiddies."

Garrett sits in the backseat, and Olivia and I sit in front and attempt to engage him in some small talk, which is a challenge. But by the time we get to Cameron's house, he seems a bit more relaxed.

"Cameron and I used to be friends," he tells us as Olivia parks in front. "Back in grade school."

"Really?" says Olivia. "You guys seem so different."

"That's probably why we're not friends anymore."

"Funny how people can change," I say as we get out of the car.

"Man, am I nervous." Olivia looks toward the brick house in front of us. "This feels worse than doing a solo at a school concert."

"Just imagine those guys in their underwear," says Garrett.

Olivia and I laugh.

"Yes," I agree. "And really bad underwear."

"Right," says Garrett. "Like tighty-whities that got washed with a red towel."

"Pink!" I say as we walk toward the house.

"Thanks, you guys." Olivia rings the doorbell, and although we can hear music coming from somewhere, no one answers the door. "Do you think this is a trick?" she asks anxiously.

"Why don't we try the garage," I suggest. "It sounds like it's coming from there."

"I'll go check," offers Garrett, which seems rather nice considering he's been sort of ambushed into hanging with us this afternoon.

"He's really nice," Olivia says as Garrett walks toward the garage.

I nod. "Yeah. He just needs some friends."

Then Garrett waves for us to join him, and before long, Olivia is introducing us to the members of the band.

"I already know Garrett," says Cameron. "What's up, dude?"

Garrett shrugs. "Not much."

"They just came to listen," explains Olivia. "Hope that's okay."

"Cool," says Cameron. "Groupies."

"We don't *need* an audience," grumbles Jack, the bass player. I remember now that Olivia had her concerns about this guy, and he does seem like a grump. But Cameron ignores him, and Dirk, the drummer, seems amused by the spectators as he fiddles with his cymbals.

"You guys can sit over there." Cameron nods to a weight bench against the wall as he hands Olivia some pages. "Here's the song we're working on. We'll run through it once so you can hear it then you can join in the vocals second time around. Okay?"

"Sounds good." But I can hear the nervous strain in her voice. Suddenly I remember that my purpose here is to pray. So with eyes wide open, I do that.

Dear heavenly Father, please help Olivia to relax and do her best. And if it's Your will for her to participate in this band, please, make it work out so that they will all want her and appreciate her. But if it's not Your will, I ask that You just close the door and lock it shut. Amen.

They band is playing now, and the sound is really pretty good. Apparently they have a keyboardist who's missing, and Olivia asks if they'd like her to step in. Cameron looks kind of surprised, and Jack looks totally skeptical.

"Sure, if you want," says Cameron. "But can you sing and play keyboard at the same time?"

Olivia makes an uncertain face like she's not too sure about this. Of course, this is a total masquerade since I'm well aware that she can play piano and sing simultaneously. She does it at church fairly regularly and sometimes at her house when we're just playing around and I'm imagining that I have some singing talent, which is a big joke.

I glance at Garrett, and he actually looks worried for her sake. How sweet is that?

"She can do it," I whisper as they get ready to start the song.

He nods but still looks concerned. I suspect he's had his own embarrassing moments. He seems like the kind of guy with an empathetic spirit too. I'm so glad he came with us today. And he actually looks pretty cool in his aviator shades. I'm thinking with a little work, Garrett could look a whole lot less nerdish. Still, I'm not sure he'd be willing. And I don't want to insult him.

Suddenly, Olivia is playing keyboard and singing into the mic, like a real pro. It's fun watching the faces of the guys. Cameron and Dirk are totally getting down. But Jack, although surprised, still doesn't look pleased. Just what is his problem anyway?

Then I notice that he does resemble the guy in my visions. Especially when he holds his head down to look at his bass. Maybe that's what this is about. Maybe Olivia was really on to something here. Whatever the case, it's fun listening to Olivia holding her own with these bad-boy dudes, who actually seem more like normal kids right now.

"That was awesome," Cameron says when they finish up. Garrett and I are clapping from our spot on the weight bench.

"You're really good, Olivia!" explodes Dirk.

"Not bad..." But Jack's voice sounds flat, and he doesn't even look at her.

"Come on, Jack," urges Cameron. "Admit that she's good. Really good."

"He won't," teases Dirk, "'cuz Jack wants to keep doing vocals."

"You're full of—"

"Then admit it. She's good," challenges Cameron.

"Yeah, man," says Dirk. "You stink at vocals, Jack. Get over yourself, okay?"

Jack lets out some foul language, and I can tell Olivia's getting uncomfortable.

"Sorry about him." Cameron frowns. "He's just jealous."

"And you can go to—"

"Lighten up, Jack," says Dirk.

"Maybe this isn't such a good idea." Olivia sets down the mic.

"See what you did, Jack?" Dirk points a drumstick at him. "You're scaring her off now."

"We don't need no girls in this band."

"Is that the problem?" asks Cameron. "'Cuz if it is, you're going to have to change your voice and sing higher."

"Maybe get a sex change." Dirk grins.

"Because we want a girl singer. If Kyle were here, he'd agree." Cameron glances at Olivia. "Kyle's our keyboardist. He's got the flu."

"And Kyle's not gonna like that Olivia's trying to replace him," Jack says.

Olivia holds up her hands. "Hey, I'm not trying to replace—"

"*Ignore* Jack," says Cameron.

"Yeah, he don't know jack." Dirk laughs at his own joke.

"Kyle plays a couple of other instruments too," says Cameron. "Do you play anything else?"

"Just flute and cello and violin, but I'm learning guitar."

"Maybe she can replace you." Jack sneers.

"Look," Olivia says in a calm tone. "I don't want to be the cause of a big disagreement. Maybe you guys should talk this over while I'm gone. And whichever way you decide to go, I'm fine. Okay?"

"Yeah, maybe we can work Jack over once you girls are out of earshot," teases Dirk. "Either he complies or he'll be singing soprano too."

"Funny," snarls Jack. "Maybe I'll just get the—"

"No!" Olivia says in a loud voice. "We're going. You guys work this out."

"I'll give you a call," says Cameron. "Thanks for a great audition."

And then we are outta there.

"Whew," Olivia says once the door is closed. "That got a little creepy."

"That Jack dude has a real attitude problem," says Garrett.

"Just because I'm a girl? What's up with that?"

"Maybe his mother used to beat him and he's a woman-hater now," suggests Garrett. "Or maybe he's just gay."

Olivia and I laugh, but Garrett gets quiet now. So Olivia and I make a few more corny jokes at Jack's expense. But then I notice that Garrett's not laughing. And I start to feel bad about making fun of Jack. What if that poor guy really is the one in my visions? What if he's depressed and suicidal? For sure, he'll be going onto my prayer list now.

"Thanks for coming with us," I tell Garrett as he's getting out of the car.

"It was cool. Thanks for asking me." Then he looks out toward the street just as a big black diesel pickup pulls up behind us, the engine revving loudly. The look in Garrett's eyes is hard to read. It seems a combination of fear and anger. And maybe even disgust. But I have no idea why.

Then the pickup pulls into the driveway, and the older guy inside gives us all a good, long, hard look before he goes into the open garage door then closes it.

"Is that your dad?" I ask lamely.

He nods. "See ya."

"Take it easy," I say. But as he walks away, head hanging slightly down, something begins to click in my brain. Something very disturbing.

Fifteen

O livia," I say as she pulls out into the street.
"I think I know who the suicide guy might be."

"Yeah? Me too!"

"Really?"

"Duh. Jack McAllister. That guy has some real issues.
I mean, at first I thought he just hated me personally. But then
I could tell he's mad at the world in general. I don't know
why, but for some reason that kid is in serious trouble. I can
just feel it. Do you think it's because of drugs?"

"No."

"But how can you be so sure?"

"I mean, *no*, because I don't think it's Jack."

"Huh?"

"When I said, 'I think I know who the suicide guy might
be,' I wasn't even thinking about Jack, although he is definitely on my list of possibilities, and I'll admit he's got some
problems. I don't get why he's so down on you, Olivia.
You really *were* awesome."

"Well, thank you." She smiles and turns the corner.

"And you could be right. Jack might be using drugs
and it might be making him act like that. Especially if he's
coming off something. Zach could get really mean and

creepy when he was coming off something. Mom used to think it was because he was *on* something. And one time Zach told me that's just how ignorant she was because he acted way nicer when he was high than when he wasn't."

"Really?"

"Yes, but I'm digressing here. I think I know who the suicide guy is."

"What makes you so sure it's not Jack?"

"Well, I realize that his actions today make him seem likely, but I just got the strongest impression that it could be Garrett."

"Garrett?" She seems genuinely surprised. "He seems so nice and normal. I really like him, Sam. I'm glad you asked him to come, and I'd like to get to know him better. What makes you think he's suicidal? Seriously, if I had to bet which guy's about to check out, I'd go with Jack. That boy's got issues."

"Obviously, Jack has problems. And to be honest, I have no idea whether or not suicide is one of them. But I'm suspicious of Garrett."

"Why?"

"It's because of a letter I read on the suicide website a few days ago. Something I almost forgot, but now I could swear that it might've been written by Garrett."

"But that website is all over the country," she points out. "Wouldn't it be quite a coincidence if Garrett was using it too?"

"I know it seems like a long shot, but some things just seem to add up." So I explain to her about the guy who wanted to kill himself because his dad was beating him up because he was gay.

"You think Garrett's gay?"

"Well, the guy on the website was gay."

"So how does that make him Garrett? I'm confused."

"The guy on the website goes by gg for Gay Guy. And gg's dad has a pickup."

"Lots of people have pickups, Sam."

"Did you see the way Garrett's dad looked at us?"

"No."

"Did you see how Garrett acted when his dad came home?"

"No."

"And Garrett had a black eye today."

"So?"

"Gay Guy, online, said his dad beat him up the other day, the night before Garrett didn't come to school. Then he finally shows up today and he has a black eye and a swollen nose. He said he ran into a door."

"Maybe he did."

"Or maybe he didn't, Olivia. And did you notice how quiet Garrett got after making the joke about Jack being gay? It's like he took it personally, but it was *his* joke."

"Yeah, he did kinda shut up after that."

"So, can you see how I'm thinking it might be him?"

"Not really."

"I've got an idea."

"What?" She's pulling up to my house now.

"Do you want to go to the game tonight?"

"Sure, but what does that have to do with Garrett?"

"We'll invite him to join us."

"Okay."

"And maybe we can talk to him."

"Like ask him if he's gay and wanting to kill himself?"

I punch her arm. "No, silly. But you could mention his black eye, since I already did. And I'm curious about his mom. I mean, if he's the guy online, I gotta wonder what's up with her, why she'd let her husband get drunk and beat up her son."

"Yeah, that's terrible."

"Anyway, maybe if we get to know him better, it'll be clearer. And if it's not him, I can focus my attention on Jack."

"And even if Garrett's not your suicide guy, he could still use some friends, don't you think?"

I nod as I open the door. "Yeah. Thanks, Olivia." Then I tell her that I'll call and invite him, and she says she'll be here around seven.

When I get home, there's a message from Conrad on our machine. I almost expect it to be an apology since he's been sort of ignoring me lately, but instead he sounds slightly irritated.

"Hey, Samantha. I tried to catch up with you after school today, but you were taking off with your lab partner. What's up with that? And why are you so busy lately? I mean, I've got basketball and there's not much I can do about that, but it's like every time I look for you, you're not there. Maybe we can talk after the game tonight."

My first reaction is to delete this message and get mad. He's accusing *me* of not being there. What about him? Then I calm down and replay the message, and I can actually hear the hurt in his voice. Like he's not sure where we stand. And I realize that our biggest problem at the moment might be that we haven't really talked for several days. And, okay, it's pretty funny, but I also think he's a little bit jealous of Garrett. Oh, well.

Then I call Garrett's number, but a man with a gruff voice answers the phone. He yells at Garrett to come get it then after some shuffling sounds, a little more yelling, and what seems an inordinately long time, Garrett finally says a glum, "Hello."

"Sorry to bother you," I say quickly. "This is Sam." I can hear his dad still talking in the background. I can't make out the words, but the tone of his voice seems angry.

"It's okay. Just make it quick."

"Olivia and I wanted to see if you'd like to come to the game with us tonight."

"Really?"

"Yeah, it's not like I'm making this up."

"Sure. When?" And he sounds so eager that I want to run over and pick him up right now—although I have no car. I seriously wonder if his dad is going to beat him up again and if Garrett is really the guy who's been writing on the suicide website. Although I know that's a leap on my part, but it seems a real possibility. Something inside me, maybe it's God, seems to be confirming this.

"Well, Olivia was going to pick me up at my house," I start saying without really thinking this through. Most of all I want to get Garrett out of his house ASAP. "So, would it be too much trouble for you to come over here? I don't live that far from you, and we could just hang—"

"Sure," he says eagerly. "That sounds good." Then he lowers his voice. "Give me the directions and I'll be right over."

"Great!" So I give him directions and hang up. Okay, what am I getting myself into? Am I crazy? Is my imagination just working overtime? Or is something really going on with Garrett? Then I literally hit my knees and ask for God to help.

Dear heavenly Father, if Garrett is who I think he is, please, help me to help him. I know this will take some divine intervention, and I really need Your assistance. Please, protect Garrett right now. Get him safely here. Then show me what to do. Amen.

Then I call Olivia and tell her what I just did. I also describe what I think the tone of his father's voice sounded like. Basically hateful and lethal. Like poison.

"So what are you going to do when Garrett gets to your house?"

"I have no idea. Any suggestions?"

"Hmmm…well, he might be hungry."

"So I should feed him?"

"Why not?"

I consider this. "Okay, maybe I'll make some spaghetti. I'm sure my mom would appreciate it."

"I'd offer to help, but I promised my parents I'd go to dinner with them before the game. My dad thinks he hasn't seen me in days, which is actually his fault, not mine."

"Pray for me," I say before we hang up. "And Garrett. I feel just like I feel in chem class, like I'm in way over my head."

She laughs. "You're never over your head, Sam. God just wants to remind you that He's the one in control. Your weakness is simply God's opportunity to be strong. You'll be fine. And I will be praying."

To my relief we do have what it takes for spaghetti. Fortunately, it mostly involves a jar of sauce and some pasta. But I dig out the parmesan cheese and find some garlic bread in the freezer. Then deciding it might be good to have a distraction when Garrett gets here, I dig out the ingredients for a green salad. This will make Mom happy.

As I work on this last-minute dinner, I pray for Garrett. And I pray for me. I ask God to help me not say anything lame or offensive. Just how does a person broach these subjects anyway? I can't just blurt out things like, "Are you gay? And do you want to kill yourself?"

Lord, please help me.

Sixteen

As it turns out, I never get a chance to ask Garrett any terribly personal questions. Mom gets home before he arrives, and I don't really want to explain the whole thing to her, other than the fact that Garrett is my lab partner and a kid who just needs a friend.

Still, she's pleased at my attempt to make dinner and even helps me with it. And then when Garrett finally does arrive, she's very congenial and kind to him. The one thing I do learn, via Mom's questions, is that Garrett's parents are divorced. His mom lives somewhere else, and he seems reluctant to discuss her much more than that.

Then Olivia gets here, and we all head off to the game. I can tell Olivia's curious as to what happened and whether or not Garrett is the guy in my visions. Finally, we both head to the bathroom during halftime, and I fill her in.

"I didn't get a chance to find out anything," I quickly explain, without revealing enough information to get the attention of other girls in the bathroom.

She nods knowingly. "Well, it's still a good thing that you did that, Sam."

"I guess." Then I tell her about Conrad's message and how I'm kind of worried. "I need to talk to him after the game."

"Let's all go out together."

I nod. "Yeah, that might help clear up some things."

The game is close, going into overtime, but McKinley wins by one point, and our team looks devastated. They do their high-five congrats with the other team, then leave the floor with heads hanging.

"Now I don't know what to do," I say to Olivia as we file down from the bleachers. She just shrugs.

"What's wrong?" asks Garrett.

"Well, I'm kind of going out with Conrad Stiles," I say. "And I wanted to talk with him after the game. But he probably isn't in a very chatty mood now."

"Oh."

"I should explain," I tell him. "I think Conrad is jealous of you."

Garrett grins now. "Of me?"

"Yeah. He saw us together after school and left a funny message on my machine."

Garrett frowns. "Funny, how?"

"Oh, just in that he sounded jealous. I think his feelings were hurt." Then I notice Alex down on the gym floor. He's staring right up at us. "Hey, I'll see if Alex can give him a message. You guys wait, okay?" Then I jog over to where Alex is standing by himself.

"Too bad about the game, huh?" he says.

"Yeah, bummer." I glance over my shoulder to see Olivia and Garrett waiting off to one side. "Could you give Conrad a message for me?"

"Sure. What?"

"We're heading over to pizza, and I thought maybe he could meet us there."

"What's up with Garrett Pierson hanging with you and Olivia?"

"He's my lab partner," I say somewhat defensively. Now I'm wondering what's up with Alex and Conrad being so suspicious of poor Garrett? I mean, these guys are Christians too. They know that we should reach out to others.

"It just seemed like Garrett needed a friend," I tell him. "So Olivia and I have befriended him. No big deal."

Alex nods. "Hey, that's cool."

"Yeah. So, you'll talk to Conrad?"

"No problem."

Then I head back to Garrett and Olivia. "Guess that's all I can do."

"Wanna get pizza?" Olivia asks, more to Garrett than me.

"I guess." He looks a little unsure, like he's still trying to figure out how he got involved with us two girls. And I suppose he seems a little suspicious, like why are we so interested in him.

But as Olivia drives us across town, we make some jokes and the atmosphere lightens up. Why have I been obsessing over this guy? He actually seems pretty normal. Maybe I'm all wet about him being the suicide guy, not to mention gay. I remind myself of what Pastor Ken said about balance.

The pizza place is already pretty packed, mostly with kids that have been at the game, but Garrett and I find a table against the wall and we stake it out while Olivia gets at the end of a long line to place our order.

"You're kind of a loner, aren't you?" I say, hoping to get him to open up a little.

"Yeah."

"So, have you always been like that? I mean, I sort of remember you from middle school, and it seemed like you had some friends."

"Like the chess club?" He grins.

"You said you were friends with Cameron."

"That was more like grade school."

"Oh."

He adjusts his dark glasses, which are still hiding that shiner.

I glance over to the counter, wishing that Olivia would hurry since this conversation could use some help, but the line appears to be frozen in time. Then I notice Cameron approaching her. "Hey, there's Cameron. He's talking to Olivia."

Garrett turns to look. "Do you think he's officially asking her to be in the band?"

"I don't know why not. I mean, didn't you think she did great today?"

"She was awesome."

I smile at Garrett, glad that he appreciates my best friend's musical talents. "But what about Jack?" I scan the room to see if he's here too. Fortunately, I don't see him. But I do see Dirk over at the soft drink dispenser.

"Jack's definitely a problem," says Garrett.

"I think he was really threatened by Olivia. But I don't get that. Do you really think he's gay? And if he is gay, would that really make him so hateful to her?"

He shrugs. "Hard to say. Maybe Jack's got a crush on Cameron and is worried that Cameron might be into Olivia." He nods to where the two of them are talking with their heads close together. I assume it's because it's so noisy in here, but it could be misunderstood as something else. *"That* could make him jealous."

I laugh. "Well, it seems slightly ridiculous. Although now that you mention it, Cameron does seem to like Olivia a lot. But she is pretty and nice. Don't you think so, Garrett?"

He gets a funny look. "You're not trying to set me up with her, are you?"

"No, of course not. But don't you think she's pretty? I mean, Cameron and lots of guys could do much worse."

Garrett nods. "Yeah, she's pretty. But so are you."

I smile. "Well, thanks. I wasn't fishing for compliments."

"And you're both nice."

"And so are you." Just as I say this, I see Alex and Conrad walk in. And before I even have a chance to wave, Conrad spots me. At first he smiles, and then he notices that I'm with Garrett and frowns. I wave anyway, motioning for him to come over here.

"Don't look now," I say quietly to Garrett, "but Conrad's coming, and I think he's still worried about you and me."

Garrett actually laughs. "Well, I'm sure you can straighten him out." Now was it just my imagination or did he put an emphasis on the word *straighten*?

"Want to join us?" I sweep my hand across the large table. "Olivia's ordering and we're just holding down the fort. Conrad, you know Garrett don't you?"

He nods. "Hey, Garrett."

Alex looks a little uncertain about joining us.

"Don't worry about Olivia," I tell him. "She's like so over you." Okay, that's an exaggeration on my part, but maybe it's necessary if everyone is going to just move on.

"I'll go order for us." Alex nods to Conrad. "I'm sure you'd just like to sit down after that game."

"Thanks." Conrad sits down adjacent from me.

"Sorry about the game," I offer.

"You guys gave them a tough go," says Garrett. "And I think that last foul call was all in the ref's head."

Conrad smiles now. "Yeah, you and me both."

"And considering that McKinley will probably go to state, you guys should be proud that you made them work so hard to win tonight. Not every team can say that."

"Yeah, but it would've been cool to win."

I give his hand a squeeze. "I know."

He smiles at me, and I think we're okay.

"So, Garrett, what's with the sunglasses at night?" asks Conrad.

"It's his new 'cool dude' look," I say quickly. "Speaking of cool, let me tell you about Olivia's audition today." Then I launch into a dramatic retelling of our afternoon. I point over to where she's still in line talking to Cameron. "We think Cameron is into her." I nod to Garrett.

"Yeah, and we think it's making Jack McAllister jealous," Garrett chimes in.

"Huh?" Conrad is clearly confused now.

I laugh. "Well, if Jack is gay, which is an unknown factor. But for whatever reason, he seems to really dislike Olivia."

"So, is she really joining their band?" Conrad asks with a frown. "And aren't they a pretty gnarly bunch?"

"I don't know if she's joining or not," I say lightly. "She and I have both been really praying about it. I mean, God does want us to reach out to others…and maybe this is Olivia's chance." As I say this, I feel Garrett's gaze on me, and I can tell he's putting two and two together and assuming that he's my special project. So I look directly at him. "And I happen to like making new friends. Take Garrett—I never really knew him before chemistry. And now that I've gotten to know him, I think he's a cool guy."

"Thanks," he mutters.

"Seriously," I continue. "Why are so many people afraid to get to know anyone outside of their little circle? I mean we're teenagers, and we're supposed to be risk-takers, right? So why do we hide inside our little comfort zones so much of the time?"

I nod back to where Olivia and Cameron are still talking. "I think it's very cool to see people knocking down walls and making new friends. Don't you guys think so too?"

"Sure," says Conrad, and I can tell he's sincere.

"Yeah, I guess," adds Garrett, as if he's actually coming around.

We kick this around some more, and finally Olivia comes back with Cameron in tow. "I'm in the band!" she announces happily as she hands us our soda cups.

"Congratulations!" I shake her hand. "You are one smart dude, Cameron. Olivia sounded great with you guys."

He nods. "I know."

"What about Jack?" asks Garrett.

Cameron kind of shrugs. "Hopefully he'll come around. Dirk and I think he was just having a bad day. He's not always like that."

"I invited Cameron and Dirk to join us," says Olivia. "Is there room?"

"If you pull in another chair." Conrad scoots his chair closer to mine. "We can squeeze together."

Before long, Alex rejoins us. And as I look around the table, I'm thinking it's really a mixed bag here. But it's pretty cool. I'm thinking that God is smiling on us. Garrett is by far the quietest in the group, but I'm hoping he doesn't feel like too much of a misfit. And it's a comfort that the guys are being pretty civilized to him. Would they have problems if they knew he was gay? Not that I know this for sure. But I just wonder.

I can tell that Conrad is tired, and I'm feeling pretty strung out myself. I nudge him and ask if he plans to go home soon.

"You need a ride?" His eyes look hopeful.

I glance at Olivia, who is actually the life of the party at the moment. Seriously, it's like, other than Conrad, she's got the attention of every guy at the table. Even Alex is spellbound as she talks about the band and some songs she'd like them to try.

"Conrad and I are going to split," I announce as we both stand. "Anyone else coming?"

Alex looks uncomfortable now.

"I've got my car," says Olivia, not directly to Alex. "It's just Garrett and me if anyone wants to hitch a ride."

"You kiddies go on home and get to bed," teases Cameron. "The big people aren't ready to turn in just yet."

So just like that, Conrad and I leave. It's still cold and damp outside, but the rain has let up. Conrad slips his arm around me and gives me a little squeeze as we walk across the parking lot. "So we're really okay?"

"Of course. But life's been crazy."

"And you're not secretly in love with Garrett Pierson?"

I laugh. "Not even close. But I do want to be his friend, Conrad. Are you okay with that?"

"Totally. I agree with your new 'love one another' plan."

"Like it's my new plan," I tease. "Remember the guy who originally introduced it?"

"Well, I like that you want to live like Jesus, Sam. That's very cool."

He opens his car door for me.

"I haven't been in your funny mobile for a while," I point out.

"My funny mobile?"

I chuckle as I climb in. "Well, not everyone has a bright orange 1976 Gremlin."

"Guess I'm just lucky, eh?"

"Or blessed."

He leans in and kisses me. "Yeah, *blessed*!" Then he closes the door, and as he walks around to the driver's side, I so want to tell him about my concerns for Garrett being suicidal and the whole Cody thing and why I've been a little distracted. I'd love to tell him exactly what's going on with me and *everything*…but I know that I can't. Maybe someday.

For now it still needs to remain a secret.

Seventeen

Hanging with Mom has never been a whole lot of fun. Okay, to be fair, it hasn't been much fun these past five years. Mom *used* to be fun. But losing Dad changed everything. Mostly Mom. Without Dad around, life got extremely serious.

But after a few years passed, things started to get a little better, Mom started to lighten up, and I felt slightly hopeful about our family. Then it all came undone again, thanks to the whole mess with Zach and drugs. That's also about the same time that Mom got a promotion and her job got stressful. Consequently, my mom has not been fun and she has not been herself—not in years.

So when I got up this morning and remembered this was our "special" day to go shopping, well, I wasn't exactly looking forward to it. Sure, it sounded like a good idea last week when we decided to do this. But as we're driving to Portland this morning, I start to replay some of our other shopping trip fiascos over the past several years—the fights we got into over clothing styles, high prices, designer labels, and whatever.

Anyway, as we enter Pioneer Square in downtown Portland, I am literally bracing myself—hoping and praying that today won't turn into one of those bad scenes that will later haunt us both on the Memory Lane of Horrific Shopping Trips.

The funny thing is, other than a few silly squabbles, which we quickly resolve, we're actually having fun. Go figure. Our main goal is to change Mom's frumpy, dated image. So we do some shopping and then pop into one of those haircut places where you don't need an appointment, and Mom gets her hair cut in this trendy layered style. And right now she's getting some highlights—like a real mini makeover!

I get my hair trimmed too, but because of the highlights, her appointment is taking longer. So I decide to go out in the mall and use this extra time to catch up with Olivia on my cell phone. I want to hear all about last night.

"So what happened after we left?" I ask. "You were like the belle of the ball."

She laughs. "It was so great, Sam. I wish you'd stayed. Although I can understand how you and Conrad needed some alone time."

"Come on, tell me what happened?"

"Well, I guess Cameron sort of does have a crush on me. And while that's really flattering, I made it perfectly clear to him that I don't really want to go out with him. For one thing, I don't think it'd be good for the band. But I also told him that, as a Christian, I've made a commitment not to date guys who aren't."

"You really told him that?"

"Sure. And he was cool with it."

"And?"

"And what?"

"What about Alex? I mean, I'm surprised that he continued to hang with you guys."

"You and Conrad didn't give him much choice."

"He could've left with us. He clearly wanted to stay. I saw him looking at you. When we were leaving, he had this slightly dazed expression going on."

She giggles, reminding me of when we were about thirteen. "Well, the funny thing is that Alex actually started to act like he wanted to get back together with me. Not that we were really dating."

"Seriously?"

"I think so. But I was just really sort of chill and aloof, you know. Not that I was being mean to him, I was just kind of, well, disinterested."

"Good for you."

"I was enjoying myself, just chatting with all those boys," she continues. "It was pretty funny, me sitting there with four guys at my table."

"Like the queen holding court."

"I guess."

"And how was Garrett? I mean, I felt sort of bad for abandoning him."

"He seemed totally fine, Sam."

"And when you dropped him home?"

"He really seemed okay. Of course, I didn't ask him if he was suicidal or homosexual or anything like that."

"Duh. And what about Alex? Did you take him home too?"

She laughs. "I think he wanted me to give him a ride, but I hinted to Cameron that Alex didn't have a car and how they didn't live too far apart. So I assume Alex rode with them."

"Too funny."

She tells me some more interesting bits of trivia, and I glance at my watch and tell her that I should probably go check on Mom. "I just wanted to make sure that everything went okay. And I guess I was mostly concerned about Garrett."

"I think you must be wrong about him, Sam."

"How can you be so sure?"

"I don't know. I just think he seems pretty normal. Although you're probably right about one thing—that guy does need some good friends. Oh, did I tell you that Alex actually invited him to youth group tonight? Can you believe it? Alex invited Cameron and Dirk too, but they said they had other plans, although that might've been an excuse. But Garrett said he'd think about it."

"Cool."

"So maybe that suicide vision really was about Jack…or maybe even Peter Clark."

I consider this as I gaze blankly into the window of a video game store. "I don't think so…"

"Well, I'm sure it'll all make sense someday."

"I hope so." I'm about to tell Olivia good-bye, when suddenly I get that flash of light. At first I think it's just a reflection from the glass window I'm staring at, but then things change, and my eyes lock on to this poster advertising a very sinister-looking video game. But the weird thing is, I can see Cody Clark inside the poster. It looks like he's trapped, like there's a glass window in front of him, making it so he can't get out. He's beating against it with his fists, and his eyes are frightened, and tears are streaking down his cheeks. I even notice the hole in the knee of his jeans.

"Oh, no!" I gasp, unable to say anything more.

"What? Are you okay, Sam? Are you getting mugged? What's happening?"

"I just had *one*, you know…" I lean against the stone column to steady myself, trying to calm down before I attract the attention of the security guard across the way. He probably thinks I'm on something.

"A vision?" she whispers.

"Yes." I take in a slow, deep breath and consider the meaning of what I just saw. Cody trapped in a video game. Not so very different from my first dream about this kid, and at least he wasn't holding a gun to his head this time. So why was it so disturbing?

"He wanted out!" I say.

"Who wanted out?"

"Olivia," I say quickly, "do you have the latest *Final Fantasy* game?"

"What?" she sounds incredulous. "What are you talking about? Are you okay?"

"Do you have that game?"

"You don't even *like* video games, Sam. Really, are you okay? Should I dial 911?"

"No, I just need the latest *Final Fantasy* game—what number is it?"

"*Final Fantasy VII*?"

"Yes, that's right. You have it, don't you?"

"Sure. But what is going on with you? You sound like you're seriously losing it, Sam. And you're scaring me."

"Sorry." So I quickly explain my vision and how I need to borrow that game and how I could use a ride over to Cody's house too. "Can you help me?"

"Of course."

"Thanks. Now I better go check on Mom. That is, if I even recognize her. She's starting to look like a whole new woman."

"Fun."

"Seriously, she looked about ten years younger just by getting her hair cut." I want to reassure Olivia that I'm really okay.

"I can't wait to see her."

"I'll call you when we get home."

It's past two when Mom and I finally sit down for lunch. She's picked a pretty cool Italian restaurant downtown.

"Dad and I used to eat here sometimes," she tells me after we're seated. "Back when we were newly engaged and I was still going to Portland State. This was one of our romantic spots." She glances around the room and sighs like she wishes he were sitting here instead of me.

"I miss him too, Mom."

She nods. "And I suppose you know what Paula says about that?"

"I'm not sure," I admit. "Should I know?"

Mom smiles. "Paula says that we're lucky to have had a man in our lives who was such a good guy that it actually hurts to miss him. Not everyone gets that, Sam."

"Oh…"

"It just doesn't make it easier."

"I know." I smile at her. "Man, you look so great, Mom. Have you checked yourself out in the last few minutes?"

Her hand flies up to touch her changed hairstyle. "I almost forgot. Is it really that good?"

"It's excellent. And that lipstick color the salesgirl recommended for you is way cool. Seriously, you look like you're in your late twenties."

She laughs. "Oh, go on. Tell me another one."

"Okay, maybe early thirties. But very cool. I can't wait to see you in that khaki suit we found for you at Banana Republic."

Mom shakes her head like it's something scandalous. "I can't believe you got me to shop there, Sam."

"Lots of women your age shop at Banana. Even Mrs. Marsh shops there sometimes. And can you believe that suit was 20 percent off?"

"That *was* nice. But how about your birthday present?" Mom inquires. "Are you happy with what we got?"

"I totally love everything, Mom. Thanks so much!"

Mom bought me some awesome pieces from The Gap. The coolest pair of jeans—I only had to try on about fifty-eight other pairs first, but the end result was so worth it. And then I found this sweet little pale blue jacket and matching T-shirt. And while we were waiting in line for the cashier, Mom insisted on getting these earrings and necklace that were absolutely perfect with the sweater. Altogether it's a very cool outfit that I can't wait to wear!

"So we still know how to have fun?" Mom asks as the waiter approaches to take our order.

"I think we do."

Later as Mom drives us home, it begins to rain, and my thoughts drift to Cody and the vision I had today. I wonder if he's all right. And okay, for a brief moment, I feel guilty for having had such a good day. But then I have to ask myself, what's up with that? Just because someone else is suffering doesn't mean that I shouldn't have a good day sometimes. And really, having a good time with my mom was probably way overdue.

Suddenly I remember what Pastor Ken said about the need for balance in my life, and I decide that was exactly what today was about. *Balance.* Does that mean I don't need to be concerned for Cody? Not at all. But at the moment there's nothing I can do to help that kid. Except pray. And that's exactly what I do.

Eighteen

By the time we get home on Saturday, I have less than an hour before Conrad will be here to pick me up for youth group tonight, and I know that's not enough time to go see Cody. Even so, I give his mom a quick call. I tell her that I was thinking about Cody and, if it's okay, I'll drop by the video game that I promised to borrow for him tomorrow after church.

"Oh, that would be nice," she says. "It might get his mind off things."

"Off what kinds of things?"

"He's been thinking about Peter a lot lately. Ever since you and Detective Hamilton were here. He seems very confused and easily upset."

"Has he told you anything new?"

"No. Just that he misses Peter. He spends a lot of time in his room. Or playing video games. I wonder if he might be depressed."

I want to say, "How could he *not* be depressed?" but she sounds so depressed herself that I hate to add to the misery. Instead I tell her that I've been praying for them and that I look forward to seeing Cody tomorrow. "But maybe you shouldn't tell him that," I say. "I don't want him to worry that I expect him to talk about anything. I just want to loan him the game he wanted."

"That's fine."

Then I decide to put on the cool outfit I got in Portland today. I put on all the pieces together, including the boots Olivia got me, and I think I look pretty hot. Then I go down and see that Mom is wearing some new duds too.

"Wow, you look awesome, Mom."

"Thanks." She smiles and does a turn that shows off her jeans. She told me that they are the first pair of cool-looking jeans that she's had since she was a teen.

"You really do look younger."

"And you look great too, Sam. I love that color on you."

"Conrad's picking me up for youth group in a few minutes." Then I frown. "What about you? You're all dressed up and looking cute, but do you have anywhere to go?"

She shrugs.

"Why don't you call Paula?"

"Oh, I don't know."

"Why not, Mom? She's single too. Maybe you guys could go to a movie or something. Just have some fun."

"Well, I suppose I could try."

I get the cordless phone and place it in her hands. "Here, Mom. Go for it!"

I can hear her talking to Paula as I get my jacket. It actually sounds like they might do something tonight. And it's fun to hear a slight lilt in my mom's voice, like she really does want to have a life. Well, this is a start. A very cool start.

I'm pleased to see that Garrett is at youth group tonight. Conrad and I get there a few minutes late, but I immediately spot Garrett with Alex and Olivia. He still has on his dark glasses, which are cute, but he definitely needs some serious wardrobe help. I wonder if he's open to suggestions. Conrad and I go over and join them at the snack table, and Olivia gives me a thumbs-up on my new outfit.

Youth group begins with what Nick, our youth pastor, calls "social hour." We mostly hang and eat and drink, and some kids play stuff like Ping-Pong, pool, or the arcade games. It's pretty relaxed and a good way for kids, especially visitors like Garrett, to loosen up. Then we get together and sing. Sometimes Olivia helps lead the songs. But she seems to have the night off tonight. Then finally Nick gives a brief, but usually very good, message.

Nick is a cool guy. He's only been youth pastor here since last fall, but everyone seems to like him. I'm guessing he's around thirty, but he seems younger. He has a goatee and a tattoo. His tattoo is on his right forearm, a cross with a crown of thorns.

Tonight he's talking about forgiveness, telling a story about when he was a teen and how he got really angry when his parents got divorced. He thought it was his dad's fault, and for years he refused to forgive him. Then he discovered that his mom had actually been having an affair. So he got mad at her and refused to forgive her.

"The funny thing was that I still considered myself a Christian during all this time," he says. "Of course, I couldn't believe my parents were still saved and acting the way they were. In my mind, they had lost their faith when they lost their marriage, and I couldn't forgive them for any of it. But eventually my heart got so hardened against my parents that I totally fell away from the Lord too. I spent my college years messing around with all sorts of crud—you name it, I probably tried it—until one night I was so wasted that I thought I was actually going to die."

He pauses for a sigh. "I think I actually wanted to die. Life had no meaning, no joy, nothing but emptiness and pain. And even though I wasn't living like a Christian any- more, I started ranting at God. Like it was all His fault. Like He was the One who'd messed up my life. I was in such a rage—and did I mention plastered?—that I put my fist through my dorm window." He holds up the arm with the tattoo and points out a scar. "And I severed an artery and nearly bled to death before my roommate came to his senses and called for an ambulance.

"When I woke up in the hospital the next day, I was a mess. Not just physically either. I felt worthless and useless and hopeless. And I was just lying in that bed, wishing that my roommate hadn't called the paramedics and that I'd died since it seemed like the easy way out. And as I was lying there, mostly feeling sorry for myself and wishing I were dead, I suddenly got this very strong sense that I was *not* alone. My heart started pounding, and I knew that the presence I felt in the room was that of the Lord Jesus. I can't explain how I knew this, but I did.

"Anyway, I just closed my eyes, and in that same instant I heard Him say, *'I forgive you, Nick. And in the same way that I forgive you, you must go and forgive others.'"* Nick just shakes his head. "And that changed everything. I rededicated my life to the Lord. And I forgave both my parents, as well as a bunch of other people. But I learned a powerful lesson about forgiveness."

He glances around the room. "Man, it's the key to *everything.* Jesus meant it when He said that we're forgiven by the way we forgive. Because when we refuse to forgive, we lock ourselves up in a spiritual prison—and forgiveness is the only key to unlock that door."

He talks a little while longer, reading the Scriptures that back up this theory. And then we pray and he encourages us to take a few minutes to search our hearts to see if we need to forgive someone.

Although it was a good message, I don't feel like it was really meant for me. I think hard, and the only people I can come up with are my mom and my brother. And it seems like old stuff that I should've gotten over with by now, but then again I don't want to take any chances. So I forgive Mom for the times she's hurt my feelings by not understanding or respecting my gift, although I'm sure I've done that before, and I'm not feeling any bitterness toward her today.

Then I forgive Zach, once again, for becoming a drug addict and making life hard on all of us. Okay, even if I'm just jumping through a spiritual hoop, at least I did it. Then we sing a couple more songs and are dismissed.

As usual, kids are invited to stick around and play games, eat food, or just visit for another hour or so, which we do. Conrad and Alex invite Garrett to join them playing pool, but Olivia and I decide just to watch. As we sit on the sidelines, I'm curious as to Garrett's response to Nick's message but don't quite know how to ask him without really putting him on the spot.

"Good shot, Garrett," Alex says after Garrett puts another ball in a pocket. "I guess I should've known that a science dude would get pool since it's mostly physics and geometry."

Garrett gives Alex a curious glance, like he's weighing that comment, trying to decide if it was meant as a slam or a compliment. But then he seems to let it go, and I'm glad for his sake. Being overly defensive never helps anyone.

"Maybe you're right about Garrett," I say quietly to Olivia. "He does seem pretty normal. Maybe he isn't the guy in my vision."

Olivia nods. "Let's hope not. Now tell me about the plan for tomorrow. Do I get to meet Cody, or do I just drop you off?"

I consider this. "Maybe you should meet him. You could even challenge him to a game of *Final Fantasy*."

"Sure. Anything to help. I've been praying for the Clarks."

I let a yawn escape as the guys finish up their pool game, but it's barely over when they decide to play another one.

"I think I'm going to head for home," says Olivia.

I glance over at Conrad. He seems to be having a good time. "Could I hitch a ride?"

Of course, that's okay with her. And I tell Conrad that the girls are calling it a night and that I'll ride with Olivia.

"I don't have to keep playing," he says.

I shake my head. "No, go ahead. I'm fine, really."

"How about a ride to church tomorrow?" he asks.

"Sounds good."

As Olivia drives me home, I lean back in the seat and just relax. I really am tired. Then just as I'm closing my eyes, I experience that flashing sensation again. My body gets tense, and I brace myself for whatever it is that God wants to show me. But all I see is red. Red everywhere. Then almost like a lens coming into focus, I realize that it's blood. And I see a dark-haired guy whose wrists have been slit. And that's all. End of vision.

I sit up in the seat and let out a little gasp.

"You okay?"

"I just had a vision," I say slowly.

"Really?" Olivia glances at me. "Right here? In my car?"

"Yes." Then I tell her about it and she, like me, gasps.

"Ugh, that's horrible, Sam. How can you stand it?"

I just shake my head. "But who is it? Who is the guy?"

"Was it Garrett?"

"I don't know. I never saw his face. Again, he had dark hair, but mostly I saw blood—everywhere. It was so gory. There's no way a person could survive losing that much blood."

"Do you think it was because of what Nick talked about tonight?" she asks. "Remember how he cut an artery when he put his fist through the window."

"Like you think that influenced my vision?" I snap at her, immediately feeling defensive even though I know there's no point.

"I don't know…"

"Sorry to lash at you. But, *no*, to your question. My dreams and visions aren't like that, Olivia."

"Sorry. I should've known that."

We're both quiet as she drives me the rest of the way home. Then I thank her for the ride and tell her I'll see her tomorrow.

As I walk into the house, I consider her question. Why did it irk me so much? Is it only because I'm tired? Or am I worried there could be something to it? Then I remember Nick's message on forgiveness and decide I better be sure to forgive my best friend.

The house seems quiet, which isn't so unusual. But for some reason I think maybe Mom hasn't gotten home yet. And when I check the garage, I see that her car is gone. Well, good for her. I hope she's having fun. Although it's after eleven, and I hope she doesn't stay out too late. I also wonder what she and Paula might be doing at this hour. Maybe they're having coffee after a movie. Well, whatever.

I'm not sure how long I've been asleep when I hear a loud crash downstairs. At first I think I'm having a dream and then I realize that, no, this is for real. *Could it be Zach?* He used to come home late like this sometimes. But then I remember that Zach is still in rehab, or he's sup-posed to be. I glance at the lighted numbers on my clock to see that it's 2:13 in the morning. And then I hear another noise. Is someone breaking into our house?

I grab my cell phone and tiptoe to the door and peek out. There are no lights on downstairs, but I can hear someone moving down there! Still clinging to my phone, I dash out of my room and straight down the hall toward Mom's. At least we can hide out together while we call the police. But when I get to Mom's room, she's not there!

Okay, what is going on here? Has Mom been abducted? I'm just starting to dial 911 when the door to her bedroom opens and the light goes on, and there, standing in the doorway, looking nearly as shocked as I feel, is my mom.

"Sam?" she sputters.

"I thought you were a burglar."

She giggles, holding her hand over her mouth. "I knocked over a lamp."

I walk closer to my mom and peer closely at her slightly flushed face. "Mom?" I say in a shocked tone. "Are you drunk?"

She giggles again. "No, shweetie, I jus' had a couple of drinks with Paula and I—

"Did you drive home like this?"

She holds her forefinger over her lips. "Shhh…you're going to wake up the neighbors."

"Mom!"

Now she frowns and almost looks like she's going to cry. "Don't be mad, Sammy."

I take in a deep breath. "I'm not mad, Mom. But I'm concerned. Did you drive home like this?"

She just grins and shakes her head. "No, no, I did not. The nice bartender man called me a cab." She laughs. "He didn't call *me* a cab. That would be rude. He called *for* a cab." She's staggering toward her bed now. I help her to lie down and slip off her shoes, then toss her chenille throw blanket on her.

"Sleep it off," I say in a stern voice. "We'll talk in the morning."

"Yesh, Mommy."

I roll my eyes as I walk back to my room. Maybe Nick's sermon on forgiveness was meant for me after all. Go figure!

get up early on Sunday morning and do damage control in the living room. I still can't believe my mom came home drunk last night. In fact, if not for the fact that there's a broken lamp on the floor and no car in the garage, I might've thought I'd simply experienced a new kind of warning dream from God.

As I clean up broken porcelain, I wonder why God didn't warn me about this. I dump the shards of blue and white into the trash can and sigh. Mom's going to be sad when she discovers which lamp she broke. It was the Chinese ginger jar from her grandmother, the one she used to always tell Zach and me to be careful of. At first I thought I could glue it together, but there were so many tiny pieces, it was hopeless.

I'm thinking about Nick's words last night, about how not forgiving his parents was his downfall. So I'm determined not to do that with Mom. I make a conscious effort to forgive her. And not to be mad or indignant.

Okay, I'm still irritated, but as I make a strong pot of coffee, I try to put myself in her shoes. I take a quick inventory of her life, and it seems to add up to problems: 1) Mom's not walking with God, 2) the love of her life was murdered and taken from her, 3) her oldest son is a recovering meth addict, 4) her daughter has dreams and visions, which she cannot understand, and 5) her job has been stressful. Is it any wonder the poor woman went out and got wasted last night?

Not that getting drunk is going to improve the status of her life, but I suppose I can understand just slightly. Still, it worries me, and I don't know what to do. Well, besides pray. And I'm already doing that.

———

"You're sure quiet today," Olivia says as she drives me to the Clark home. "Did I offend you last night when I said that stupid thing about your vision? I'm sorry. I think I was just tired."

"No, that's not it at all." I tell her about Mom's late night antics. Okay, it's a little embarrassing telling your best friend that after your mom had a makeover that makes her look young and cool, she suddenly starts acting like a teenager on a drinking binge.

"I feel like it's my fault," I admit. "It's like I wanted her to have fun and have a life. I encouraged her to call Paula. Who knew they were going to go barhopping?"

Olivia actually laughs. "It is *not* your fault, Sam. And if I know your mom, she probably feels horrible right now."

I kind of chuckle. "Actually, she does feel horrible. But that's from the hangover."

"Yeah, well, when the hangover's over, I'll bet you that your mom will be really sorry."

"I guess."

"Let's pray for Cody," says Olivia suddenly. "I have a feeling God is going to use you today, Sam."

"Okay." Not that I feel terribly usable at the moment, but then God is God—so who knows? So we pray, and Olivia asks God for a miracle. I agree and we both say amen, and then we're there.

I feel nervous as we walk toward the house, so I continue to pray for Cody. I'm wondering if I'll get a chance to really say something meaningful to him today. Or if I should even say anything without having Ebony here. Then again, I have a feeling Ebony would encourage me to get the boy to talk.

Mrs. Clark lets us in then disappears, I assume to her bedroom. I introduce Cody to Olivia and produce the coveted video game, and he suddenly brightens.

"Want to play it now?" asks Olivia, sitting on the couch right next to him.

"Sure."

So they pop it in and soon are playing. Olivia explains some things, but Cody seems pretty comfortable, so she just encourages him and gets into it.

Okay, I'm starting to feel a little bored after nearly an hour of this, and I say to no one in particular that I'm going to go downstairs to the basement. I don't even know why I really want to do this since it pretty much creeped me out the last time. But maybe it's like facing my demons. Or maybe I'm just really bored. If nothing else, I figure I can pray.

Everything looks the same down here, and I get that same chilled feeling again. I mean, obviously it's cold since it's February and raining outside. But it's more than just that. It's almost as if there's a real spiritual force down here, and I have half a mind to drag Olivia down here so we can both pray over this room, the way she did for my own bedroom after we visited the suicide website. Maybe I will.

I walk around the room, looking at not much of anything, and I almost expect God to show up and give me a vision—maybe that final vision that will make everything make sense. Then I hear footsteps, and I nearly jump out of my shoes. But I turn to see that it's only Cody.

"What are you doing down here?" he asks in a suspicious voice.

"Just thinking. Where's Olivia?"

"Using the bathroom."

"Oh."

"What are you thinking about?"

I decide to play my hand carefully. "Your brother."

"What about him?"

"I'm thinking that he didn't really kill himself. I'm thinking that he'd like to have the truth told."

Now Cody doesn't say anything, just stands there halfway down the stairs with a frightened look on his face. I almost expect him to turn around and bolt.

"I know you're afraid," I continue in a quiet voice. "And I can understand that. But I also know that you loved your brother, right?"

"Yeah."

I look right into his eyes. "Your brother would want you to tell the truth, Cody. He wants you to know that it's the right thing to do and that you will be okay."

"How do you know that? I know you had that dream and everything. What are you? Some kind of psychic or something?"

I don't react to this accusation, but for some reason I feel like I need to tell him the truth. "I have a gift, Cody. A God-given gift for knowing and seeing things. But no, I'm not a psychic. It's not like that." I pause. "And do you know what?"

"What?"

"I had a vision about you yesterday."

He comes down the steps now, slowly, but I can tell he wants to know. "What was it?"

"You were trapped in a video game again."

"Uh-huh?" he peers at me with interest.

"But you wanted out."

"Huh?"

"You were trapped," I explain, "just like you're trapped in this thing with Peter. And you want out, don't you?"

He nods.

"Will you tell me what happened, Cody, if I promise that I'll help you out of this?"

"Are you *really* a police officer?"

"I'm just starting to work with the police," I tell him. "But I can guarantee you that Detective Hamilton will do whatever it takes to assure that you'll be okay if you tell the truth, okay?"

"I don't know…"

"There's a verse in the Bible. It says, 'You will know the truth and the truth will set you free.' Don't you want to be free, Cody?"

He nods, and tears bead up in the corners of his eyes.

"You can trust me, okay?"

Then he starts blurting out a story, like he can't get the words out fast enough. And it all makes perfect sense. Peter's best friend, Brett Carnes, wasn't just doing meth; he was selling it too. Apparently Peter found out that Brett had sold meth to his girlfriend, Faith, getting her hooked, and Peter was furious.

"Peter kept saying to Brett, 'You lied to her, you lied to her.' Peter was so angry that I thought maybe he was going to kill Brett. But I didn't know that Brett had Dad's gun."

"And you were hiding down here the whole time?"

"I'd snuck down here to use Peter's PlayStation. I wasn't supposed to because I didn't ask first, so when I heard them coming, I hid over there 'cuz I didn't want Peter to get mad at me." He points to a dark corner back behind the stairway.

"And they didn't see you."

"Not until after." He takes in a breath. "Peter said he was going to call the cops and tell them that Brett was a drug dealer. Then Brett told Peter he wasn't gonna let him do that. He said he'd kill Peter first. But I thought they were just talking, you know?"

I nod. "Like when you get mad at someone and say, 'I'm gonna kill you'?"

"Yeah, like that. And then I heard Peter say, 'Where'd you get that gun?' and his voice sounded weird, like he was really scared. Then Brett said it was Dad's, and Peter cussed. He told Brett to put it back. He said he never should've showed Brett where Dad kept the gun. But Brett said it was too late. Then Peter started begging him, and I didn't know what to do. I thought maybe Brett was just kidding. Maybe he was trying to scare Peter to keep him from calling the police. Then I heard the shot." Cody starts to cry harder now.

"It's okay, Cody. Peter would be glad you're telling the truth."

"Brett heard me under the stairs. I think I was crying. And he came over and told me that Peter had just killed himself. And I told him, 'No, you killed him.' Then Brett got really mad and pointed the gun at me. He said, 'I think Peter killed you too. Yeah, he killed you and then he killed himself.' And Brett held the gun to my head."

"Oh, no!"

"He told me to keep my mouth shut or me and my parents would be just as dead as my brother."

"What did you do after that?"

"I left the house. I got on my bike and I rode as far as I could go. And then after a long time I rode back. I thought maybe it didn't really happen, maybe I'd just been playing a video game and that I imagined it happened. I thought Peter was still alive. But when I got here, he was dead."

"And you never told anyone what really happened?"

"I was afraid of Brett. He started coming over here all the time after that. He acted all nice and like he was my new big brother, and my parents really liked him. The more time went by, the more I knew I could never tell. I almost started to believe that Peter really did kill himself, that Brett was telling the truth. And I thought if I told anyone what really happened, they might even blame me for it, like if I'd done something maybe Peter wouldn't be dead."

I put an arm around his shoulder and give him a hug. "I can understand that. It was really brave to tell me this. Do you feel better now?"

He nods and wipes his eyes with the cuff of his over-sized sweatshirt.

"Now I'm going to tell Detective Hamilton what you told me, and I promise that you and your mom will be safe. Do you believe me?"

He nods again. "Yeah."

"Do you think you're ready to tell your mom this story?"

"I guess."

"She really needs to hear it."

"But what about Brett?" he asks with fear in his eyes.

"Brett has been a suspect already. We're pretty sure that he's not even in the state. But now he'll probably be caught and charged with murder."

"And locked up?"

"Definitely."

Cody lets out a long sigh, and I notice that the door is slightly ajar upstairs. I think I see the toe of Olivia's shoe there. I'm guessing that she's been listening and praying. And for that, I'm thankful.

"Let's go find your mom."

Then we sit down with Mrs. Clark, and with some encouragement and coaching from me, Cody retells his gruesome story. And before long she is hugging her brave young son and telling him not to worry and that everything is going to be okay now. I can see the relief in her face. Sure, this doesn't bring Peter back. But at least she knows he didn't take his own life either. That is worth a lot.

"I need to call Detective Hamilton." I excuse myself so I can make this call outside in private. She sounds stunned but pleased when I tell her the story.

"I thought it might be something like that," she finally says. "But without Cody's testimony, we had nothing. I can't believe you got him to talk." Then she laughs. "Well, actually I can. Now I'm going to call Detective Ramsay and tell him to issue a warrant and to make sure that Cody and his mom are both safe. Okay?"

"Sounds good to me."

"Good work, Samantha!"

"Thanks."

When I go back in, Cody and Olivia are playing the video game again. But Cody looks different now. Instead of a frustrated, frightened little boy, he looks like a regular kid. Even so I decide to have a private conversation with Mrs. Clark about the violent video games that Cody seems so addicted to. I go into the kitchen and express my concerns.

"I've never liked those horrid games," she admits. "But it seemed to be one of the few things Cody was interested in. Maybe we can move on now…now that the truth has come to the surface." Then she thanks me again and even hugs me. "Maybe it's time that Cody and I started going to church again."

I tell her that sounds great, and as Olivia and I drive away from their house, I know that God has begun a real miracle in their family!

———

On Monday afternoon, Ebony informs me that Brett Carnes was picked up in Idaho over the weekend. As it turned out, he was stopped for a driving violation and later charged with possession of illegal substances and illegal arms and stolen goods. Of course, the heftiest charge was added this morning, that of first-degree murder in Oregon. His bail is set at a million dollars, and he is definitely locked up.

"I told the Clarks the good news," Ebony tells me when I meet her at the station. "Cody made a statement for me just a few minutes ago. He's still here if you'd like to see him."

"I would."

To my surprise, Cody gives me a hug.

"Can I speak to Cody privately?" I ask Mrs. Clark, and she just nods with teary eyes.

Cody and I go into Ebony's office and sit down. "You know what I told you yesterday, Cody? About how God gives me visions and dreams?"

He nods. "It's true, isn't it?"

"Yeah, it's true. It's just that it's kind of a secret. It's easier for me to help solve crimes and things if no one knows about it. But I figured I could trust you. You seemed like you were good at keeping secrets."

He grins. "I am. And this is a good secret."

"It is." I squeeze his shoulder.

"I won't tell."

"Thanks."

"And my mom told me that you were worried about the video games I play," he says in a more serious voice.

"Yeah. Those violent games don't seem very good to me—especially when I saw them in my visions."

"Anyway, I told Mom that I'd get rid of some of the bad ones."

"And your mom said you guys were going to go back to church," I say hopefully.

He makes a face. "I told her I'd go to church as long as I don't have to dress up nice."

I smile. "Lots of churches don't make people dress up."

He nods. "Good. Because God is going to have to take what He gets with me."

I laugh. "And that's just what He wants, too."

Twenty

During the next couple days, life seems to fall into a somewhat normal routine. Well, depending on how you define "normal." But I feel lighter somehow, and even the sun is shining. Of course, this only gives everyone false hopes that spring might be around the corner.

Garrett and I have been helping Olivia to make decorations for the Sweethearts Ball. Olivia even left us to our own devices yesterday since she had to practice with Stewed Oysters. It was her second practice with them, and she seems jazzed about it.

"So how's Jack?" Garrett asks Olivia in a flat voice.

"He seems to have adjusted." She cuts out yet another red heart, which I will soon be decorating with a glitter pen.

"Are you guys still planning on being the relief band for the dance?" I ask.

"I think so. Although I told the guys we wouldn't be able to pay much, which made Jack growl, but I'm willing to give up my cut. I think the exposure for the band will be good."

"And it'd be fun to see you guys perform. What're you going to wear?"

"Cameron thinks I should go with a retro look like Blondie or Madonna, you know how they used to dress back in the eighties. Kind of over the top. Would that be weird?"

"I think it'd be fun," I say as I doodle with the glitter. "As long as it's not sleazy."

"What are you wearing?"

"I'm not sure. Mom wants to go with me tonight to look for something."

Olivia tosses me a glance.

"Yeah, I guess she thinks she owes me one." I already told Olivia about how Mom apologized to me for her drunken disorderly disaster—and how I forgave her. Hopefully it'll never happen again.

I glance over to where Garrett is wrestling with the metal heart arch that we'll attach balloons to. "How about you, Garrett? What are *you* wearing to the dance?"

He gives me a totally blank look. "Who said I'm even going?"

"You *have* to go," says Olivia. "You're on the dance committee."

"I got bullied into this," he grumbles. "I never said I'd actually go to the dance."

Now Olivia goes over and stands next to him. I can tell she's about to turn on the charm. "Please, come to the dance, Garrett," she pleads with clasped hands.

"And do what?"

"Hey, I don't have a date," she says suddenly. "Sam's going with Conrad. Why don't you and I go together?"

"Are you serious?"

"Yeah," she says with bubbly enthusiasm. "It'll be fun. But you have to wear something cool, okay?"

He frowns. "Cool...like what?"

Olivia presses her lips together, and her forehead furrows. "I'm not sure. But I'll think of something. Trust me."

"Nothing too weird, okay?"

"Not too weird. But it's got to be retro since I plan on wearing something from the eighties and I want your outfit to go with mine."

Now Garrett brightens and I think maybe he's going to get into this. And why shouldn't he? Olivia is cute and singing in the band. Talk about a great opportunity for a science geek. Okay, I didn't mean that. But Garrett should be counting his blessings. I just hope he doesn't develop some kind of crush on Olivia because I can't quite imagine her getting serious about him. Then, of course, there's her no-dating-of-non-Christians rule.

As promised, Mom takes me "formal" dress shopping, and after several pathetic stores that seem to specialize in ugly, weird, or sleazy, I tell Mom I want to go to Ross Dress for Less.

"You're kidding?" she says. "You used to hate that place."

"Well, I hate these places too," I say as she drives away from the formal wear shop. "Maybe I'll find something funky at Ross. Olivia is going retro. Maybe I can find something that's a little wild or off beat, maybe something I can fix up to look different. Plus, it'll be cheap. And all I told Conrad is that I'll be wearing red."

So we hunt and hunt at Ross, and I finally find a sort of interesting fire engine red dress that's way too big. But we borrow some straight pins from the dressing room lady and play with the dress a little, taking it in, pushing up the sleeves, and then Mom finds a wide shiny belt and some red platform sandals. I think I'm set.

Okay, it's a little flashy, but if Olivia's going for drama, then maybe I can carry it off too. Besides, this is supposed to be fun. It's not like someone's getting married or something.

"You really don't mind altering the dress for me?" I ask Mom as we go home.

"No, I think it'll be an easy fix, and that belt is going to help a lot too."

"Thanks." Then I lean back and close my eyes, imagining what fun we'll have on Saturday night. Just normal kids doing normal—

Then here it comes again, a flash of light and suddenly I see a somewhat familiar scene. It's exactly the same bridge as I saw several weeks ago, the one near Kentwick Park. Only this time, it's not cloudy and gray outside. Instead, the sky is clear blue and I don't see anyone on the bridge. I think this is God's way of reassuring me that the original suicide vision and the subsequent ones don't really mean anything. Maybe it's over. Like a big sigh of relief. But in the same instant, I see a guy walking along the bridge again, slowly walking, as if he's afraid he's going to fall, *as if he's afraid of heights*. And then I see his face—clearly—and it's Garrett. No doubt, it's Garrett.

"Oh, no!" I slap my hand over my mouth.

"What?" asks Mom, and I can tell I scared her. "What's wrong?"

"Sorry," I say quickly. "I was just, uh, I remembered something."

"What?"

"Just homework," I say, which isn't untrue. "A project I'd almost forgotten about."

"Oh."

As soon as we're home, I run upstairs and turn on my computer. And for no explainable reason, except that I feel compelled and it might be a God-thing, I go straight to the suicide website. I don't even feel that surprised to see there is a post from *Gay Guy*.

I'm giving up. This time I mean it. You guys probably won't believe me, but then I don't think we believe anyone until the deed is done. So you're probably wondering, What is it now? Why is Gay Guy finally ready to throw in the towel? I'll tell you why. It's because I'm fed up. I've really been trying to live a regular life lately. Just like someone from this site advised me to do. I didn't get counseling, but I did make some friends. Friends that my dad keeps questioning. He thinks they must all be gay like me. Why else would they want to be with me? And when I told him I was taking one of my friends, one who happens to be a girl, to the

Valentine's dance, he laughed right in my face.
He said no self-respecting girl would want to
be seen with someone like me. He said she must
be a desperate lesbian, and I told him to take it
back. Big mistake. He knocked me around some,
and then I really stood up to him. I told him I
was done with him and that I was sick of him
and that I was going to do something about it.
He just laughed. And each time he laughed it
felt like being stabbed, and I realized that he's
been slowly killing me for months now. That's
when I knew I was done. Tomorrow is the day.
Good-bye, suckers. Hope you'll figure it out for
yourselves too. It's hopeless. Totally hopeless.
Why stick around? gg

I know this was written by Garrett. I have no doubt. But I don't know what to do about it. I consider calling him right now, but it's getting kind of late. And okay, what if I'm wrong? Or what if the phone call sets off his dad again and puts Garrett in an even worse position? But then again, what if Garrett's in danger right now?

I pause to pray, asking God to guide me, and that's when I remember the vision again. The sky was clear and blue, like it was the middle of the day. I have to trust the vision. I have to trust God. If this is for real, I have at least until tomorrow. Still, I know that I need to pray for Garrett. I need to pray God's protection over him tonight. So I call Olivia and tell her what's up.

"Tomorrow we intervene," I tell her. "We'll find Garrett before first period, and we'll sit him down to talk. We'll stop this thing before it's too late."

"Right. In the meantime, we pray."

By morning I feel like I've barely slept. And it would be easy to feel really nervous. Instead I pray. And I'm thankful I didn't have any new dreams. Maybe that means so far, so good.

On the way to school, I call Ebony and leave a message on her voice mail. "I am 99 percent sure that the suicide guy is Garrett. Olivia and I are going to try to talk to him ASAP, but I'm not sure what to do if he doesn't listen. Anyway, I'll be in touch."

Then we're at school, but we don't see Garrett anywhere. We ask Alex and Conrad, and they haven't seen him either, but then that's not so unusual. It's not like Garrett goes around trying to be seen by everyone.

"I have geometry with him," says Alex, "in second period."

"Great," I say. "Tell him we need to talk to him. It's urgent."

"Yeah," adds Olivia. "It's about the Sweethearts Ball. We have a real disaster on our hands."

Alex buys this and promises to give him the message. But Olivia and I decide to take it a step further and agree to meet at the math department after second period. "That way we can talk to him sooner," I say. "In case he gets suspicious after Alex tells him about our 'disaster.'"

"Sorry," says Olivia. "I couldn't think of anything else."

"It's okay. And, in a way, it's true. If Garrett goes through with this, you won't have a date."

She winces. "See ya after second."

But when we find Alex by the entrance of the math department later, he informs us that Garrett is absent today.

"Oh, no." I turn to Olivia.

"Just what kind of decorating disaster is it anyway?" asks Alex. "Maybe I can help."

"No, that's okay." I grab Olivia by the arm. "Can you drive?"

And then we're on our way to Garrett's house. I'm calling him as she drives, but no one is answering. "He might be there," I say. "Maybe he's just not picking up."

But when we arrive and beat on the door, there is no answer. We try the side door. Still no answer.

"We need to go to the bridge," I say as we run back to her car. "And I'm calling Ebony."

As Olivia speeds to the bridge, I can't help but notice that the sky is clear and blue. Just like in the vision, which I assumed was later in the day. Why did I assume it was afternoon? It could be morning just as easily.

I get Ebony's voice mail again and leave another message, explaining what we're doing, what I think is going on, and where we're headed.

It seems to take forever to reach the bridge, and then we don't know where to park. It's a railway bridge with no direct access unless you're a train. Finally, we park near the boat ramp and start walking toward the bridge.

I don't see anyone around, and there's no car, but then I remember that Garrett doesn't have a car. Doesn't even have access to one. Gay Guy couldn't use carbon monoxide poisoning since his dad kept the pickup keys from him. My guess is he walked here—it would take a couple of hours from his house.

"Look," Olivia says in a hushed tone and grabs my arm, pointing to the bridge. And that's when I see him, exactly like my vision, walking slowly, shakily, as if he's very, very scared.

"Garrett," I whisper. "Please come down." Of course, he can't hear me. He's too far away.

"What do we do?" asks Olivia.

"Here." I hand her my cell phone. "Call Ebony. Hit number one on my speed dial. Tell her that he's up there right now and that I'm going up too. Hopefully no trains are coming anytime soon."

"Oh, Sam."

"And pray."

Then I scramble up the side of the graveled hill. I try to be quiet, but I'm afraid the rocks slipping beneath my feet might give me away. Hopefully the sound of the fast-moving river will cover for me. Below the bridge is a mix of rapids and large stones. The water is so shallow that if a person did survive the jump, he would probably be crippled for life.

Soon I'm on top of the bridge, trying to convince myself that heights don't bother me or that this isn't dangerous. Now I'm walking across the bridge, taking one tie at a time, trying to get into a pace, a rhythm, and trying not to look down where I can glimpse white water and stones between the ties. I think the ties are far enough apart that a person could fall through, although perhaps if you spread your arms, it might keep you from going all the way down. But who can be sure?

My plan is to get close enough to Garrett so we can talk. Somehow I have to get him to trust me, to listen, and to see that this isn't the answer—that there is hope. Most of all, I don't want to scare him. I know that he, like me, is afraid of heights and one quick move... Well, I can't think about that now.

He has stopped walking and is now just standing with his legs straddled, one on each tie, like he's frozen. Maybe scared stiff. I quietly continue toward him, silently begging God to help me, to help us. Finally I'm only about four ties away, and I can't believe he hasn't looked back. He's still frozen, and I have to admit I feel like freezing too. I feel like crying for help. Instead, I take in a steadying breath and quietly say his name.

Of course, this makes him jump, which makes me jump. My heart is pounding like crazy, but I try to remain calm. "It's just me. Sam," I say in an even voice. I'm close enough to see that his legs are really shaking. "It's going to be okay, Garrett."

He just stands there with his back to me, like he really can't move. And yet he's moving all over. He's shaking so hard that I think he might vibrate himself right off the bridge. Like there may be no way to help him. Then it occurs to me—what if a train came right now? Would it even have time to stop? Don't think about that!

"Garrett," I say as calmly as I can muster, although I can hear the tremble in my voice. "Is it okay if I walk up closer to you? I'm, uh, I'm kind of scared right now."

I think he says okay, and so I proceed—with caution. Extreme caution, and I think I might be shaking as much as he is. I reach the place where I'm parallel with him, and then I go ahead and walk right past him, just a couple of ties ahead since I think he might need his space. Or maybe I'm afraid he might grab me and we both might go down.

I attempt to steady myself as I try to think of something to say. "Nice day." Okay, it's lame but the best I can do under the circumstances.

He doesn't say a word, doesn't even look at me, but his face is so white that it seems all the blood has drained out. Perhaps he is dead already.

"Want to sit down?" I carefully squat and then sit, which actually feels a little safer. I let out a sigh. "Much better."

But he's still standing, one leg out in front of the other and both legs still shaking like reeds blowing in the wind.

"This is a pretty scary place. Especially if you're afraid of heights."

His eyes narrow slightly, but he still doesn't look at me.

"Why don't you sit down, Garrett. Give your legs a rest."

"I can't," he mutters his eyes still looking down.

Now I stand back up. "Do you want me to help?"

"I don't know."

"Can I walk toward you?"

He doesn't say anything, but something about his expression makes me think this might be okay. I pray it's okay. The last thing we need is to panic. I slowly move along the ties until I am standing next to him. "Now I'm going to sit down," I say as if I am talking to a little kid. "Right here. And then I'll reach for your hand, and you can sit down too. Okay?"

He doesn't answer, but after I sit and reach for his hand, he takes it. His hand is clammy and cold, and after what seems like an hour, he finally sits down and heaves a huge sigh.

"Isn't that better?"

His head is bent down and he's still not talking.

"Garrett, I know that you're gay. And I know your dad is abusive. And I know you want to give up."

He turns and finally looks at me. "How do you know that?"

"The suicide website. I'm Grace. Olivia is Hope."

He seems genuinely surprised by this but only says, "Oh."

"We're your friends, Garrett. We want to help you. I didn't actually figure out that you were Gay Guy until just last night. I mean, I had my suspicions, but when I read that post about the dance, I knew it had to be you."

He barely nods.

"But this isn't the answer."

"There are no answers."

"Yes," I tell him, "there are. God has an answer for everything."

"I thought God hated homosexuals."

"God loves everyone."

"That's not what I heard."

"Well, do you believe everything you hear? Do you believe your dad when he says the kind of crud he says to you? Does he really know what he's talking about?"

He shrugs.

"The truth is, God does love you, Garrett. I know this for a fact."

"A fact?" his voice is dripping in skepticism. "A fact requires proof, Sam. Don't forget that I'm the scientific one here."

"I know it for a fact because I have faith."

It gets quiet now, and I hope that he's considering this.

"How did you find me here anyway?" he suddenly asks. "I never mentioned this place on the website or to anyone."

I point a finger at him. "See, that in itself is *proof.*"

"How?"

"Because God showed me where you were."

"Yeah, right."

"I swear it's the truth, Garrett. God really did show me."

He gives me a look like he thinks I'm even crazier than he is.

"God has shown me all kinds of things about you."

"Like what?"

So I actually go into the details of the many and varied suicide visions I've had just recently. "I'm not sure if you actually tried any of these methods, or if you were simply considering them. But God knows our thoughts, Garrett. And for some reason, God tuned me into yours. I believe He did that because God really, really loves you and wants to save you from this."

Then I tell him about how I felt lost when my dad died. "I needed a father badly, and I discovered that God wanted to be that to me. He's my heavenly Father, and I can honestly say that I wouldn't want to live without Him. I'm pretty sure that's why you don't want to live now. You're doing it on your own, Garrett. Without God. Without your heavenly Father." I don't add that it doesn't help much that his earthly father is being such a jerk.

Garrett gets so quiet that I'm not sure whether he even heard me or not. But then I see something wet glistening on his cheeks. He's crying.

"We have to get down from here."

"I'm afraid, Sam."

"It's okay," I tell him as I stand. "I'm afraid too. But we can help each other. Just trust me, okay?"

It takes a few minutes and lots of coaxing, but he finally stands up again. Then, holding hands, we take the ties one at a time and, ever so slowly, make our way back to terra firma, which I want to kiss but don't. Then I throw my arms around Garrett and give him a big hug. "It's going to be okay. You're going to get past this." He's still shaking, but at least he doesn't resist. In some ways he seems beaten, and I have a feeling he thinks he's failed again. But at least he's alive. Now he has a second chance.

As we go down the graveled slope toward the park, I notice Ebony's car parked next to Olivia's, and the two of them are standing together. Not far off is a marked patrol car as well as a paramedic unit. I guess they were getting ready for anything. I'm glad they didn't use sirens or anything.

"That's Ebony Hamilton," I explain as we get closer. "She's a good friend of mine, and she's also a cop."

He bristles slightly at this.

"You're going to have to trust me on this. And her. We want to help you. Okay?"

His eyes narrow. "How?"

"For starters, you need a new place to live. I'm pretty sure Ebony will agree. Your dad is abusive and cruel. And that's wrong."

He nods ever so slightly, but his head is hanging low. I suspect he's ashamed, although that seems absurd.

"Things are going to change for you, Garrett. But you need to accept some help, okay? Can you do that?"

"Yeah, I guess."

Then I introduce him to Ebony, and she talks to him for a few minutes, asking him some questions, which I assume are to establish that he's currently not a threat to himself or anyone else. Then she points to the patrol car. "Normally, you would be transported in that, but if Samantha's willing to join us, you can ride with me to the station."

"That's fine," I tell her.

Then Olivia comes over and gives Garrett a big hug. "I'm so glad you're okay. I thought I'd lost my date to the Sweethearts Ball."

"So that's what this is about," he says, displaying enough humor to give me hope. "Man, you are one desperate chick, Olivia Marsh."

She just laughs then says she'll meet us at city hall. Garrett and I get into the back of Ebony's car, and she drives to the station, where I'm sure he'll be questioned some more. Olivia pulls up as we're getting out of Ebony's car. We all go inside, and Olivia and I talk to Garrett for a while. Then Ebony returns, thanks us for our help, then says that she needs to get a statement from him.

We both hug Garrett before we leave. "I'm so glad you're getting help," I tell him. "It's going to be okay now. It's going to get better. You'll see."

He still looks doubtful, but not nearly as scared as he was on that bridge. He tells us good-bye and then even adds, "Thanks."

"See ya later, Garrett." Olivia pats him on the back.

He looks skeptical. "Yeah, see ya."

"Count on it," I tell him.

"Did Ebony tell you that a train was scheduled to go through there while you guys were on the bridge?" Olivia asks when we get into her car.

"No, are you serious?"

"Yes. Ebony called the railroad and told them to delay the train until you guys got safely down."

"Wow." I try not to imagine what might've happened up there today. "Let's pray for Garrett," I suggest. And so we do.

———

On Saturday night, the night of the Sweethearts Ball, Conrad and I double-date with Olivia and Garrett. We've already spent about five hours getting all the decorations up, with barely enough time to go home and change. I went ahead and told Conrad a little bit about Garrett, not all the details, but just enough to make him understand how important it is for us to stick by Garrett, especially now.

Garrett's in a foster care situation, which he says is "a Christian home, but sort of okay," plus he's getting counseling regarding his sexual orientation, which he seems a little unsure about. In fact, it almost seems that it was more the result of his dad's bullying than anything else. But I am not pressing him on the subject. I'm just glad that he's still here and still talking to us.

He's been back at school the past couple of days, and although I can tell he has still got some obstacles to face, he's certainly turned a corner. Olivia and I both are convinced of this. It's like he's a different guy now, like some heavy load has been lifted off his shoulders.

Just today, as we put up decorations, he was joking and cutting up more than ever. He thinks it's a hoot that Science Geek is taking Rocker Chick to the Sweethearts Ball. And Olivia has done a great job putting their outfits together. They look totally retro and fun.

All in all, it's a great night. Olivia and the Stewed Oysters are a bigger hit than the main band, and Olivia is fantastic. Of course, Jack still looks like he's got an ax to grind with her, but Olivia just takes it in stride.

I'm sure this new side of her surprises a lot of people. Alex is particularly impressed, and I have a feeling he's going to be hitting on that girl again. Although she politely reserves most of her attention when not singing for Garrett, who turns out to be quite an adept dancer and rather charming.

Conrad and I have fun together too. And I love how he really treats Garrett like a friend. It probably makes me respect him even more than ever.

But seriously, the highlight of the evening for me is when I dance with Garrett. The dance is nearly over and we're all tired and happy. And I, for one, am ready to call it a night. The dance is just ending when Garrett starts to speak.

"Sam…" He looks at me, then looks away. "I don't even know how to thank you…you know, for everything."

I smile at him. "Don't thank me, Garrett. Thank God!"

"Yeah, I think I might be sort of moving in that direction."

I blink in surprise. "Seriously?"

"I can't make any promises, but I'm looking into it. Like any good scientist, I have to examine all the evidence."

"That's great, Garrett."

"Anyway, thanks for everything you've done for me, Sam. Thanks for caring. And thanks for accepting me, you know, just the way I am." He shrugs. "You know, whatever that turns out to be."

Then I stretch up and kiss him on the cheek. "I love you, Garrett. You know in a brother-sister kind of way. But I really do love you just the way you are. Just the way God loves us."

He nods. "Thanks."

And as we finish the dance and go back to join our friends, I feel totally amazed. And I realize that only God can make me feel like this. And I thank Him!

My eyes sting from the heat. I blink and rub at them, trying to see what's in front of me, but there's so much smoke I feel blind. And there's a nasty acrid smell that burns in my throat as I attempt to breathe. It smells like something that I shouldn't be inhaling. I try to hold my breath as I stumble along. I know that I need to get out of here—*fast!* But then I trip over a wooden crate, falling smack down onto what feels like a filthy cement floor. It's sticky and grimy with, I'm guessing, years' worth of crud ingrained into the surface.

Despite the filth I think maybe I'm safer down here. I recall a fireman, back when I was little, telling our class that the smoke isn't as bad if you stay low. So I continue searching for my exit, crawling on my hands and knees. The air has gotten so thick that it feels like I'm fighting my way through a heavy curtain of murky darkness.

I pull the neck of my T-shirt up over my face in an attempt to cover my nose and my mouth. I can't see a thing except for the eerie red glow off to my left, and I know that I need to get away from that—it's dangerous, deadly, and evil.

I must keep moving in the opposite direction of the fire. My time is limited. Shards of broken glass cut into my hands and knees as I creep along, and I keep bumping into things like cardboard boxes and plastic bottles and other sorts of unknown debris cluttered all over the place. It seems as if someone has been in here throwing things about, creating a huge mess that has become my obstacle course…or perhaps my death trap if I don't get out of here.

I can't give up! I continue navigating through my smoky prison. There must be a door in here somewhere. If I got into this place, there has to be a way out. I just wish I could remember where it is. I inch my way forward upright on my knees now, my arms outstretched and flailing in front of me. If only I could find a wall to follow along. Something that will lead me to a door or a window.

The heat is almost unbearable now. It feels like the back of my shirt is melting into my skin, like my lungs are about to collapse. And the putrid stench makes me want to vomit. I suddenly wonder if this is what hell would feel like—and how could anyone endure such torture? Is that where I am right now—in hell? But why? Why would I be in hell? Why would God allow that?

Finally my hands feel something solid, and it seems to be a wall. I rise to my feet and quickly use the rough wooden surface to guide me. Splinters pierce my fingers, but that's minor compared to the burning heat and the deadly smell.

I work my way along this wall until I reach what I think is a window. It's about three feet from the floor and feels as if a heavy canvas-like cloth is covering the glass. I tug at the cloth, but it's securely attached by what seem to be nails. Why would someone nail a window covering down?

Then I hear a loud sizzling, crackling noise behind me, from where I know the fire is increasing by the second. It's a menacing sound…almost demonic, like it wants to devour me, to burn me alive. I pound my fist against the cloth over the window, hoping that somehow I can loosen this covering and force open the window and—

I hear an ear-splitting explosion, and a blast knocks me off my feet and smack into the window.

When I come to my senses, I am lying facedown outside. I don't know how much time has passed, but I'm on some pavement that's cool and damp, probably from a recent rain. I can tell that it's night by the darkness and the streetlight several feet away. The wetness of the ground is such a welcome relief after the inferno I just escaped—that horrible explosion that I felt certain was going to kill me.

But when I slowly roll over onto my back and open my eyes, I see by the glow of the streetlight that what I thought was water is actually my own blood. Bright red blood is flowing everywhere. It's like a river of blood coming straight out of me. My arms and legs and entire body are sliced and shredded, probably a result of that explosion and crashing through the window.

I become dizzy from looking at my own pool of blood, or perhaps it's simply from the loss of it. No human could possibly survive so much blood loss without medical assistance. Without help, I will die.

I attempt to scream, but my voice feels small and weak. The street is completely vacant and quiet, not a car or pedestrian in sight. There is no one who can possibly come to my rescue.

"Dear God," I sob, "please, please, help me! Help me!" Then I lean my head back and close my eyes, preparing myself to die because I know it won't be long now. It won't be long...

"Samantha!" I feel someone shaking me. "Samantha!"

I open my eyes once again, and there is my mother's face hovering over me with a worried expression. I blink and sit up, realizing that I am safe and in my own bed. I look down at my arms and see that I'm not cut. I'm not bleeding.

"Are you okay?" Mom sits next to me on the bed. "I heard you screaming in your sleep. Sounds like you were having a pretty bad dream."

I'm still trying to catch my breath, to slow down my heart rate.

"Are you okay?" she asks again.

I nod.

My mom's face grows even more troubled now. "Was it one of *those* dreams?"

I know what she means by 'those' dreams. I also know that she'd probably rather not hear about it, but I'm still so shaken, so frightened, that I need to talk. "I don't know. All I know is that it was horrid."

"Do you want to tell me about it?"

I frown. "Do you really want to hear?"

She sort of shrugs. "I'm awake...you might as well tell me."

So I describe the dream to her, and her frown lines grow deeper as she listens. "That really was awful. Do you think it means anything?"

"I really don't know, Mom. I mean, I never saw anyone else in the dream. Usually those dreams are warnings for someone else. But it's like I was all alone in this one."

"Well, surely, you don't think something like that could happen to you, do you?"

"I suppose the warning could be for me, and if I ever got into a situation that felt anything like that, well, I'd probably remember this dream and get out of there before things got worse."

Mom lets out a frustrated sigh, pressing her lips together, and I can tell that I've pushed her beyond her comfort zone.

"The important thing to keep in mind," I tell her, "is that when God gives me prophetic dreams, it's almost always to help someone or to prevent something bad from happening."

She just shakes her head. I can tell she doesn't get it, doesn't want to get it, and I'm guessing she'd like to go back to bed. "Isn't there a good chance that it was simply a nightmare, Samantha?"

"Maybe..."

"Can you go back to sleep now?" She glances at my alarm clock. "It's not even four yet."

"Yeah, I'll read my Bible for a while." I force a smile for her benefit. "That always makes me feel better."

"Okay." She leans over and kisses me on the forehead. Something she hasn't done since I was little and she used to put me to bed. "Hope you have some better dreams now."

"Me too."

And although I try to appear brave and like I'm perfectly fine, I am haunted by the reality of that dream. It felt like the real deal to me. And yet how can I know for sure? And if it really was from God, what does it mean? Was it meant for me or somebody else?

Reader's Guide

1. Early in the story, Samantha begged God to give her a break from her special gift, but when He did, she got worried. Have you ever asked God to give you a break from something? Explain why and what happened.

2. Why do you think Samantha was feeling stressed when Ebony asked her to help in the Peter Clark case? Should Sam have done anything differently? Explain.

3. Were you surprised at what Sam discovered when she visited the suicide website? What are your thoughts on suicide? How do you think God feels about suicide?

4. If you suspected a friend was considering suicide, what would you do or say to help that person?

5. What do you think about the dating relationship between Samantha and Conrad? What do you like or dislike about it?

6. Did you think it was important for Samantha to talk to her pastor about her unique gift as well as her employment opportunity with the police force? Why or why not?

7. How did you feel about Samantha's mother when she came home drunk? If you were Samantha, how would you have dealt with it?

8. What were your first impressions of Garrett Pierson? Do you know anyone like him? If so, how do you interact with that person?

9. Garrett seemed confused by a lot of things, including his sexual orientation. But Sam and Olivia pretty much accepted him for who he was. Do you think that was right or wrong? Why?

10. Do you think Sam was taking too big of a risk when she went onto the railroad bridge to talk Garrett down? Why or why not?

SO YOU WANT TO LEARN MORE
ABOUT VISIONS AND DREAMS?

As Christians, we all have the Holy Spirit within us, and
God speaks through His Spirit to guide us in our walk with
Him. Most often, He speaks through our circumstances,
changing our desires, giving us insight into Scripture,
bringing the right words to say when speaking, or having
another Christian speak words we need to hear. Yet God,
in His sovereignty, may still choose to speak to us in a
supernatural way, such as visions and dreams.

Our dreams, if they are truly of the Lord, should clearly
line up with the Word and thus correctly reveal His character. We must always be very careful to test the words,
interpretations of circumstances, dreams, visions, and
advice that we receive. Satan wants to deceive us, and he
has deceived many Christians into thinking that God is
speaking when He is not. So how do we know if it's God's
voice that we are actually hearing?

First we have to look at the Bible and see how and
what He has spoken in the past, asking the question,
*Does what I'm hearing line up with who God shows
Himself to be and the way He works in Scripture?* Below is
a list of references to dreams and visions in Scripture that
will help you see what God has said about these gifts:

- Genesis is full of dreams and visions!
  Check out some key chapters: 15, 20,
  28, 31, 37, 40, 41

- Deuteronomy 13:1–5
- Judges 7
- 1 Kings 3
- Jeremiah 23
- Several passages in the book of Daniel
- Joel 2
- The book of Ezekiel has a lot of visions
- There are a lot of dreams in the book of Matthew, specifically in chapters 1 and 2
- Acts 9, 10, 16, 18
- The whole book of Revelation

If you want to learn more and have a balanced perspective on all this stuff, you'll probably want to research the broader category of spiritual gifts. Every Christian has at least one spiritual gift, and they are important to learn about. Here is a list of books and websites that will help:

- *Hearing God's Voice* by Henry and Richard Blackaby
- *What's So Spiritual about Your Gifts?* by Henry and Mel Blackaby
- *Showing the Spirit* by D. A. Carson
- *The Gift of Prophecy in the New Testament and Today* by Wayne Grudem
- *Are Miraculous Gifts for Today?* by Wayne Grudem
- *Keep in Step with the Spirit* by J. I. Packer
- http://www.expository.org/spiritualgifts.htm

- www.enjoyinggodministries.com. Click on Theological Studies Section and choose Controversial Issues. Check out Session 03-04 and 18.
- www.desiringgod.org. Click on Online Library and choose Topic Index, then check out Spiritual Gifts.

(Note: If you're doing a Google search on spiritual gifts or dreams and visions, please make sure you type in *Christian* as well. This will help you weed out a lot of deceitful stuff.)

As you continue to research and learn about spiritual gifts, always remember: The bottom line is to focus on the Giver, not the gift. God gives to us so we can glorify Him.

> "Signs and wonders are not the saving word of grace; they are God's secondary testimony to the word of his grace. Signs and wonders do not save. They are not the power of God unto salvation. They do not transform the heart—any more than music or art or drama that accompany the gospel. Signs and wonders can be imitated by Satan (2 Thessalonians 2:9; Matthew 24:24), but the gospel is utterly contrary to his nature. What changes the heart and saves the soul is the self-authenticating glory of Christ

seen in the message of the gospel
(2 Corinthians 3:18–4:6).

But even if signs and wonders can't
save the soul, they can, if God pleases,
shatter the shell of disinterest; they can
shatter the shell of cynicism; they can
shatter the shell of false religion. Like
every other good witness to the word of
grace, they can help the fallen heart to fix
its gaze on the gospel where the soul-
saving, self-authenticating glory of the
Lord shines. Therefore the early church
longed for God to stretch forth his hand
to heal, and that signs and wonders be
done in the name of Jesus."

—John Piper, *Desiring God*

Diary of a Teenage Girl Series

Kim

Enter Kim's World

JUST ASK, Kim book one

"Blackmailed" to regain driving privileges, Kim Peterson agrees to anonymously write a teen advice column for her dad's newspaper. No big deal, she thinks, until she sees her friends' heartaches in bold black and white. Suddenly Kim knows she does *not* have all the answers and is forced to turn to the One who does.
ISBN 1-59052-321-0

MEANT TO BE, Kim book two

Hundreds of people pray for the healing of Kim's mother. As her mother improves, Kim's relationship with Matthew develops. Natalie thinks it's wrong for a Christian to date a non-Christian, but Kim isn't so sure. However, when her mom's health goes downhill, can Kim wait to find out what's meant to be?
ISBN 1-59052-322-9

FALLING UP, Kim book three

It's summer, and Kim is overwhelmed by difficult relatives, an unpredictable boyfriend, and a best friend who just discovered she's pregnant. Kim's stress level increases until a breakdown forces her to take a vacation. How will she get through these troubling times without going crazy?
ISBN 1-59052-324-5

THAT WAS THEN..., Kim book four

Kim starts her senior year with big faith and big challenges ahead. Her best friend is pregnant and believes it's God's will that she marry the baby's father. Then Kim receives a letter from her birth mom who wants to meet her, which rocks Kim's world. Can her spiritual maturity make a difference in the lives of those around her?
ISBN 1-59052-425-X

Log onto www.DOATG.com